Green Tea To Go

Stories from Tokyo

GREEN TEA TO GO

Leza Lowitz

Press | Printed Matter

GREEN TEA TO GO

Published by Printed Matter Press/SARU Press International
   Printed Matter Press
   Yagi Bldg. 4F. 2-10-13 Shitaya, Taito-ku,
   Tokyo, 110-0004 Japan
   info@printedmatterpress.com
in association with Wandering Minds International

Layout & Design by Joe Zanghi & studio z
Cover design by Michele Weatherbee and Stefan Gutermuth.
Cover photo copyright 2003 by Stefan Gutermuth.

Printed in Japan
Distributed in Taiwan & the U.S.A. by SARU Press International
sarupress@yahoo.com
9F-5, #57 Sichuan Rd. Sec.1
Panchiao, Taipei 220 Taiwan

ISBN 0-935086-32-3

ISBN 4-900178-24-1

For Shogo, lover of tea

Contents

The author gratefully acknowledges Alison Anderson, Paul Bailiff, Abigail Davidson, George Evans, Leonard Gardner, Peter Goodman, Helen Taschian, Suzanne Kamata, Shogo Oketani, Donald Richie, Ken Rodgers, Richard Ruben, Moto Shibata, Drew Stroud, Susan Trott, Steve Vender, Michele Weatherbee, Hillel Wright, Joe Zanghi, Daisy Zamora, Matthew Zuckerman, Nina Zolotow, and the late Gina Berriault for their editing and guidance; as well as the editors of the publications in which some of these stories first appeared, sometimes in different form. Their support kept me going.

"The Tale of Genji: Or Glass in the Face (In Which a Girl's Love of Scars Sours)" appeared in *Japanzine*, 2004.

"The Hatchback" appeared in *Wingspan*, All Nippon Airways In-Flight Magazine, August, 2003 and as "The Pinto" in *Yomimono* #10, Hiroshima, Japan, Winter, 2003.

"The School of Things" appeared in *Wingspan*, All Nippon Airways In-Flight Magazine, March, 2003.

"Post Restante" was excerpted in *The Louisiana Review*, 2003.

"Green Tea to Go" appeared as "Different," in *Wingspan*, All Nippon Airways In-Flight Magazine, July, 2002; and in *The Dickens*, Copperfield's Books Literary Review, Volume 4, No. 1, Winter, 2000, Sonoma, CA.

"Lighthouses in the Pond," appeared in *Yomimono* #9, Hiroshima, Japan, Spring, 2000.

"The School of Things," appeared in *Japanophile*, Spring, 1999 and received First prize in the Japanophile Fiction Contest, 1998.

"Innocence," appeared in *An Inn Near Kyoto: New Writing by American Women Abroad*, New Rivers Press, 1998.

"Thirty-Six Views of the Imperial Wedding: (A Small Fable in Homage to Donald Barthelme)," appeared in *Rooms*, Winter, 1998.

"Ghost Stories" appeared in *The Broken Bridge: Fiction from Expatriates in Literary Japan*, Stone Bridge Press, 1997.

"Reply to Anything," appeared in *Prairie Schooner*, Summer, 1996.

"Sayonara, Tokyo," appeared in *Printed Matter*, Tokyo, Winter, 1991.

"Notes on Love" received a PEN Syndicated Fiction Award in 1989 and was broadcast on National Public Radio's The Sound of Writing, 1990 and published in *Edge*, Tokyo, Autumn, 1990, where it received a fiction award.

"Figures of Speech," appeared in *Transfer* 55 (San Francisco State University's Literary Magazine), Spring, 1988; and in *Sequoia* (Stanford University's Literary Magazine), Summer 1989.

She considered the demands of reality as something to be entirely crushed in favor of love, that obedience to reality meant a weakness in love. Reality was the dragon that must be killed be the lover each time anew.

—Anais Nin, *A Spy in the House of Love*

If I want to imagine a fictive nation, I can give it an invented name, treat it declaratively as a novelistic object, create a new Garabagne, so as to compromise no real country by my fantasy (though it is then that fantasy itself I compromise by the signs of literature). I can also—though in no way claiming to represent or to analyze reality itself (these being the major gestures of Western discourse)—isolate somewhere in the world (faraway) a certain number of features (a term employed in linguistics), and out of these features deliberately form a system. It is this system which I shall call: Japan.

—Roland Barthes, *Empire of Signs*

Notes on Love

At first, it starts like this: There is a couple. Say there is a woman, skin and bones and brains and passion, and there is a man. They meet, not in some crowded college lecture hall or on a ski slope but in a more pedestrian way. In transit. Home from work, or combing the streets at some odd hour, the hour of disappearances and thick airs, morning stillness, the indecision of people not quite willing to give up on a lonely evening.

This woman, she sees this man on the street, thinks she recognizes something familiar in his eyes. She decides she'd like to sleep in his arms, him holding her. She decides to trust her instincts, to follow her heart. Much later, after they have been living together for years, her lover will hold their first meeting against her, as circumstantial evidence of her impetuousness. How could she meet a stranger on the street and take him to her home? How could she have slept with a man about whom she knew nothing? Not even his name? What kind of judgment does a woman like that have? And if she slept with him, why wouldn't she do the same with other men? The litany is predictable, obvious, laughably true. There is nothing she can say.

At night, in bed, she tells him the story she heard about Christopher Columbus, how when he was a child he held an orange in his hands, turning it over and over, feeling the smoothness of the circle in his palms. A white butterfly flew up behind the orange, its wings cutting the sharp circle. Instead of wings, Columbus saw in his mind's eye the sails of a ship. The world must look similarly, he thought. It must be round.

The world is still round, she tells her lover. *It is a circle of possibilities, an endless horizon of adventure. Round and around and around again. A million revolutions in the sky.* She cuts smooth arcs in the air with her hands as she tells him the story. His eyes follow her hands, growing wide with worry. She laughs at him, until he mentions a woman with whom he had made love (or did he say: had sex) for hours/days/weeks, until they had burst out of their skins, the hours at once irretrievable and yet somehow never forgotten, alive in his mind, to be recreated at any given moment. *Like that?* he asks, picking his words slowly like blackberries. *Is my love round too? Does it come back to me like a boomerang, a double helix?*

She laughs nervously and says of course, his love is not immune from circularities, all the while the fire of jealousy burning inside of her. She will tell herself it is ridiculous for her to be jealous of someone she has never met, especially since she had just made love with the man in question. But, it is unimportant in light of this new information. It is the thought of another woman that makes her jealous, makes her dislike the theory of circles.

He puts his arms around her and nuzzles his face into her back, pretending that he still loves her. She looks in her old junk-shop mirror on the dresser, combing her hair behind her ears like Louise Brooks. She looks deeply at her own face, so intently that her own face disappears and she thinks she sees other faces, far more beautiful than hers, passing before her like ghosts. If only mirrors could speak, she thinks. Would they tell her who had been sleeping in her bed when she was gone? Her lover quotes Joni Mitchell, saying he doesn't like weak women because he gets bored too quick, and he doesn't like strong women because, you know....

She wonders which one she is.

A couple of detours. That's what her friends call them, in kinder moments. She holds her thoughts close to her body like a purse when they go out to dinner, making small-talk along the way. The content is unimportant, it could be anything. It usually is. What matters is that they eat spicy food to remind them that they are each alone in their own deserts and there is but one glass of water between them. Communication becomes a matter of survival. If she wants the glass, she will have to ask for it. Or she will have to steal it. No matter which. Procuration is a function of necessity. She is used to evasion. The thought of sharing, sadly, does not occur to either of them.

This was once the stuff of passion, she remembers. It was once a rush of pent-up energy, and the law of thermodynamics tells her that pent-up energy is released proportionate to the force that contains it. When they go home, they will make love and she will have three consecutive orgasms in a world that demands of her twelve. He will have one in a world that demands of him one. He is pleased with himself, yet convinced he has somehow failed to satisfy her. The expectations are inequitable, but she will try not to think about it. She is not even sure that he hasn't failed to satisfy her, or if it even matters. Can anything satisfy her, really?

When you are in love, he once told her, it is axiomatic that you take chances. When was the last time they had taken any chances with each other? Once, he had tied her up with striped shoelaces he had taken out of his red Converse high-tops. All the while they were having sex, she kept thinking of the laces, and how after they were through, he would put them back into the shoes. Somehow, a part of her would travel with him that way, in and out of alleys and dark, smoky clubs. Where would she go? What would she see? she wondered. Who was he when she was not there to watch him?

He told her that all relationships are doomed because we fall in love with the image of ourselves that our lover has. Once the lover discovers the reality of us, the reality seeps in and we are left with who we really are and who they really are—and who she really is, he is convinced, is a fugitive of herself. Who's running from whom? she wants to scream, but she doesn't. Instead, she tells him that she is not in love with an image of him, hoping to hear the same from him. He says nothing, looking at her reflection in the mirror.

★   ★   ★

At a dinner party in her lover's honor she sits sandwiched in between two people one, a distinguished professor of Rhetoric who suffers from perennial psoriasis, the other, a visiting female law student from Italy who happens to look like Sophia Loren, with whom she takes an instant and irrational dislike bordering on hatred. In the dinner-table patter, the men talk and joke freely as the women sit silently, popping up every now and then like small kernels of popcorn asking the hostess can they help? Clear or serve?

She wears black to the dinner. The Rhetoric professor asks her why she prefers darkness. She blushes. Sophia Loren says she thinks that black is no longer fashionable in America, that the primary colors are trend. "Trendy," she wants to say, carrying the "eeee" out in a long scream like a banshee, but she doesn't. She restrains herself. Sophia Loren asks her if she agrees that black shows a total lack of imagination. Is it a statement against interpretation? She looks at this woman's bright red blouse, the color of blood, of aggression, of passion. How can she tell her she has read her thoughts? How can she tell her that she doesn't want to be understood, or interpreted, or noticed, even. She wants to disappear, like the invisible ink of the promises he had made her when they first met.

She says that, *yes, she is in mourning.* She mourns the four-door sedan with its luxurious front seat, reduced to scrap-iron and junk heaps. She mourns the decline of the American family, which can be attributed to nothing less than the invention of bucket seats. She tells the incredulous beauty that her family used to have a big American car, and that all four of them: her mother, father, brother and she, had fit into the front comfortably. When her family had gotten a compact car with bucket seats, things fell apart. The stick shift was the least of what came between her parents she tells the Italian, mouth agape.

The professor is smiling stupidly, at her. He knows she is full of shit. He asks her: *why is it that you never see pictures of politicians smiling?* He is rubbing her knee under the table. Smiles are aggressive, she says with conviction, staring at the twitching lips of her Italian nemesis. *And politicians are sneaky,* she says with equal certainty. *Look at the bared teeth of this dinosaur.* She picks up the papier-mache candlestick on the table and raises it over her head like a club. Her lover is twirling his pasta around and around his fork in concentric circles, leaving a hole in the center of his plate, staring down.

Revolutionaries don't smile, do they? the professor asks. *Has anyone ever seen a picture of Che Guevara smiling? ...Not I,* her lover says, eyeing the Italian's chest as she breathes. When the professor asks the Italian beauty if she's ever read Aristotle, and the woman asks, *Onassis?* She smiles at her lover as if to say you get what you deserve, but her lover is smiling at the Italian woman, enraptured. The professor of Rhetoric speaks of Aristotle's three kinds of lifestyles: that of reason, that of honor, and that of appetite. He mentions this because he's leaning towards the latter and who knows how appetite can change a man. The hostess mistakes his meaning and refills his plate with steaming pasta.

But his appetite is of a different order, and she pretends not to notice the professor's hand creeping up her leg. She thinks of herself as a female version of Andrew Carnegie: a woman of iron, with nerves of steel, who can hold back a train of men if she wanted to. She can generate enough steam and energy to power a locomotive that will take her away from here. In her mind, she is lying in the top bed of a sleeper car rubbing lemon on her elbows to keep them soft. *What is it that attracts you to me?* the professor whispers in her ear. Here, as an expert in the uses of language, he knows that it will be what she says, or fails to say, that is important. She, as an expert in the art of evasion, ignores him, for he is begging the question.

When she finds the letter in her lover's desk drawer, smelling of female and lion and mozzarella, she reconsiders. It is a drawer she is never to have looked in, a drawer upon which betrayal and trust are written like the graffiti of a

drunken man. It is a drawer, like memory, which is better left
unopened...

*But I think of you when I'm here, listening to music, wondering
what you're doing. Smell this paper. Ahhhh...does it smell like me?*

She locks herself in her room, refuses to answer the
phone, counts the hang-ups on her answering machine like
sheep. Her best friend comes over, beats at the door with her
fists like a lion tamer. They sit nude on the roof of her apartment in Chinatown, watching the world below. People are
selling electronic watches and colored marbles, tv's, radios; hot
things. High above the world of commerce, they are talking
about love. Each time you are in love, your heart opens up a
little more like the aperture of a camera. It's such an old song
by now. He obviously has a guilty conscience. Why didn't you
suspect it? How could you not know that was why he suspected you?

She is hearing nothing of her friend's questioning, for she
has known all along. Instead, she is imagining her lover and
Sophia Loren in Venice, sitting over an espresso in a cafe
where love leaves its mark everywhere, like the watermarks of
floods on the city's crumbling walls. She imagines the two of
them sitting, watching the faded fishing boats break up the
water, watching the parade of old fat couples who wear their
lives together like espadrilles, worn and unraveled but too
comfortable to discard.

When her friend leaves, she turns on the television,
where Vanessa Redgrave and Timothy Dalton are performing
"The Taming of The Shrew." O Vanessa, the way she moves
her body, her presence on the stage, her movements...this
power is what she wants! She wonders why her lover has
taken up with the Italian, wonders if love for him is just a

question of exploring another's world and then when our curiosity has been satisfied, when the land is no longer interesting or exotic, the body no longer mysterious, the face somehow old and familiar, we move on to some new territory.

He apologizes, say he'll stop seeing the Italian woman, mentions marriage under his breath, like a stymied laugh at a funeral. He asks her if she could start all over, what would she do differently? She tells him the story of a couple she knows, a couple he might even recognize.

*   *   *

At first, she says slowly, it would start like this: There would be a woman, skin and bones and brains and passion, and a man. They would meet, not in some crowded college lecture hall or on a ski slope but in a more pedestrian way. In transit.

This woman, she would see this man on the street, thinking she recognized something familiar in his eyes. She would decide she'd like to sleep in his arms, him holding her. He'd take her home, and before she climbed into bed with him, she would cover the mirror on his dresser with her scarf so that no trace of her would be left when she was gone. They would make love, slowly and passionately, and she would imagine that she was an explorer, on some sort of mecca by herself. She would be climbing an endless snow-capped mountain. A man would whoosh down the mountain on a toboggan, just when she was convinced that she was all alone. He would tell her that he was not there to save her.

In her dream, he would say he could offer her warmth and companionship if she needed it on her journey. She would thank him and continue her ascent by herself, until she came to a plateau where many flags were stuck in the snow, flags from all over the world.

He would take one of the flags and wrap it around her, the colors of its rainbow surrounding her. He would hold tightly onto the flag and release her, and she would fly into the air like a kite. The wind would carry her around and around in circles. She would hear the man telling her that she was a peacock, fanning her beautiful wings behind her, unable to see or appreciate them. Turn and see! Turn and see! He would yell from the mountain, promising to show them to her. This time, she would not turn to find herself in him. She would know that if she looked back, she would tear her wings and never fly again.

So she gets on a plane and flies.

To Japan.

"Innocence"

The huge black crow on the balcony of the thirty-sixth floor of the Keio Plaza Hotel was saying something to Emily in the fading afternoon sunlight through a light rain. She had just surfaced from the crowded Shinjuku underpass, which had been as silent as an underwater tunnel, and now this. Twenty years earlier, a famous movie star had jumped from the balcony just before evening rush hour on his 32nd birthday. Now the lone black crow perched on the ledge and cawed into the sky above the din of construction. What was it saying? She was trying to make it out when a man in a dark suit careened into her and mumbled gruffly, deliberately blocking her passage with his briefcase. *Sumimasen*, she apologized softly, bowing. Walking in Tokyo required concentration; looking for the open spaces in a land where space was scarce and openness was not a quality to be admired. Then she walked on into the thick air of power of the world she did not belong to and steeled herself against the crowds. She was realizing that she did not have to belong.

The suicide had been a popular TV actor who had played macho roles, and who in real life had kept a male lover many years his junior. His suicide note spoke of his love of Mishima and said, "Father, I will wait for you in Nirvana."

She wondered if her English student, Inoguchi, knew of the actor or the suicide, but she doubted he had paid much attention to the incident. As for her, she considered it her job to be aware of things like that, the underside of a culture. Even her own. She knew about all the artists, writers, rock stars who'd left before their time. She wanted to know everything, all the time. It was easier to keep track of the people who were no longer with us than those who were. But she knew one thing for sure, that Inoguchi would be waiting for her.

She'd been in Tokyo three years and was still fascinated by how things worked. Effortlessly, yes, but somehow heartlessly. Then sometimes she'd get the feeling there was a whole world underneath, like when the cherry blossoms were falling from the trees and the drunken revelers sat half-singing, half-crying on their cardboard boxes underneath the fading beauty, or when the crows started to caw their hysterical blind cries as if from a graveyard and no one else seemed to hear them, or when someone bumped into her and she liked the combat. It wasn't life they were celebrating; it was more like people determined to be cheerful at a wake. No, it was the pain of loss. Ever since they'd lost the war. That's what the line was, anyway, but the young people didn't buy it anymore. They no longer needed a reason.

There was a small wooden house wedged between the high-rises, maybe a hundred years old. Rain traveled down the small copper chains that hung from the corners of the house to catch the water and train it down to fall in cups shaped like lotus flowers. Even nature could be tamed. But it could transcend its course and mesmerize.

The wind whipped around between the glimmering chrome and glass towers, sending spirals of paper and cigarette butts spinning in small cyclones at her feet. It had a cold beauty to it, this city, and all the sharp edges made it all the more electric for its having rebuffed the ones who tried to get close to it. In that, it was almost human. And the people still kept trying.

She knew this because there was always some new building going up in Tokyo, even with land prices soaring and the economy in the dumps. This time it was the city hall complex, whose mirrored walls and marble bathtubs would make Gotham City look like some quaint end-of-the-century charterhouse. They were working all day and all night, these men without shirts, their brown bodies sweating in beads down to their purple and blue jodhpurs with knee-high black *jikatabi*, soft socks with rubber bottoms they wore as shoes.

When she passed the soft yellow lights strung along the overpass, they seemed to her like lanterns of a boat lost at sea. She was entranced by the men who lived their lives in the darkness, digging at the earth, carving out yet another place for progress, somewhere, somehow. If they could find room for another new building in Tokyo, there was room for anything. Even for her.

She smoothed her pants as the doors to the hotel's lobby opened noiselessly in front of her. To her left, a man in a blue suit entered and exited the revolving door within half an inch of the glass. Here, in this city, such precision became a kind of mystery. She wondered if Inoguchi minded her being late as she took the elevator up to the fifth floor, which was really the fourth floor. Here, elevators did not list the fourth floor because *shi* which meant "four" also meant "death." It was unlucky to have an elevator stop for death, so they just renamed it. It did not, therefore, exist. Did Western hotels lack thirteenth floors? Or did they just override the superstition? Maybe she was too superstitious, too aware. Her mind

needed to slow down, but Tokyo was hardly the place for
that. She should have moved to Hawaii.

She bowed again, this time to the receptionist, who
cupped her hand over her mouth as she giggled and waved
the *gaijin*, the foreigner, in. The girls at the reception desk
always giggled when they saw her, because they didn't know
who she was but they figured she must be someone because
she got to be in a room twice a week with a famous movie
star, who, though happily married, had a thing for her so
strong you could sense it—like the first rumbling of an earthquake when you're not quite aware what's happening but you
know that something is off, something's about to go down. So
they sat a little straighter, waited a little more intently, felt a
little more alive, valued those minutes all the more. Then,
they laughed. They didn't much like her, but were frightened
by her.

Besides, she didn't seem to care what anyone thought of
her, and then there was the fact that her "English student"
followed her around like a schoolboy and even carried her
bags when they left together (where did they go?) and that
was something not many Japanese men did for anyone, especially famous and handsome men like Inoguchi Masao—who
didn't have to. But maybe he was just being polite. That was
his job.

When she got to the room, she closed the door behind
her, glancing over her shoulder at the girls who quickly
turned away, blushing. Inoguchi was studying the script, cir-
cling the difficult words with a cartographer's precision and
tapping his foot under the table to the beat of some imaginary
linguistic drill pounding the proper accent and syllables into
his brain.

"Hi," he said shyly.

"Sorry to be late."

"No problem. I got some time to practice my lines."

She smiled warmly. It was hopeless. It always was. It wasn't that she thought one couldn't learn a foreign language as an adult—she thought one could. But that wasn't the reason all the housewives and middle-aged men "studied" English. They wanted to learn "American." What was that, anyway? There were as many different Americas as there were Japans. Learning English, she decided, was a lot like learning to love. One only really felt love's power when it was hopeless. One only felt the power of language when one couldn't understand what was being said. She had felt it many times.

There were two bottles of Perrier on the table and two cups of coffee in Wedgewood cups getting cold. The tape recorder was red-light ready for action and a small electric heater radiated warmth from the corner. Inoguchi always brought the water, one for each of them. One must be a magic potion, the other poison, she thought. At any given time she could take the wrong one...

In the conference room next door she could hear the faint applause following the rambling speeches of promoters and businessmen toasting the start of the World Boxing Association Championships which were to open at the Tokyo Dome, the egg-shaped stadium in the heart of the city, next week.

Everyone, including Inoguchi, had their eyes on Owada, a young welterweight whose time was said to have come but whose irascibility and lack of discipline could get the better of him when it always seemed to matter the most. His father had died a mysterious death about a year ago, and he had been unpredictable ever since. He was scheduled to fight some rich pretty boy with a glass jaw and a body to die for, a fighter whose name no one knew, but it didn't seem to matter at all as far as the purse was concerned. The bets were on. And since they were fighting in Japan, he would undoubtedly win if it were a points decision.

Owada was all over the place—vitamin drink commercials, charity sports meets, government fund-raisers. She had seen him fight and had felt that tinge in the bottom of her stomach. He had something. To her, what made Owada exciting in the ring was not the lesser chance that he'd pull through—that was what everyone banked on—but the fact that he might get cocky and really blow it. Being a hundred percent hard-boiled loser was easy, but playing the hard-knocks underdog required a particular kind of tenacity and guesswork, a special kind of psychology that kept your fans wanting you to win even when they knew in their hearts you'd probably let them down again. Owada, like any good underdog, had it both ways. The fans enjoyed it when he did lose, they felt they got their money's worth anyway and were ready to bet on him again just to prove their own capacity of judgment. They'd say, "he had a bad night." Anyway, losing was noble if you'd tried your best. Trying your best was an art form in Japan. They even had a verb for it. *Ganbaru*. Go for it. It was untranslatable, but it was a word heard far more often than *sayonara*, at least in her world.

She saw her reflection in the shiny wood table and ran her hand across the surface to distract herself. Inoguchi's head jerked back slightly. He'd been looking at her.

The Japanese used *hinoki*, a light, pure cypress for the Noh stage, too. But this was not a stage, only work, and when she looked at his shoulders, strong from years of professional baseball, swimming and now martial arts, she began to reconsider. She was lonely, in the way that a lifeguard at the beach could feel his isolation. His presence was required, but not needed. Just like hers.

Inoguchi wore a black cotton turtleneck and smooth wool army-style pants in a deep army green. She threw her bag on the table, pulled out the script and sat down in the swivel chair without blinking an eye. His watch was on the table, flat, face up. A gold Tag Heuer diver's watch with an inscription on the inside thanking him for his fine work in a film about the yakuza gangs from a famous American director. He had shown it to her the night they met, when a friend of hers had given her the job and she had taken it knowing not the first thing about acting or how be a vocal coach but only wanting to be in the hub of things, where something might happen. So here she was. But nothing was happening.

"How are you?" he asked in practiced English, looking not at her eyes or her briefcase nor even the script but directly at her lips, if just to see them break out in a smile at him, at something he said.

She smiled slowly and said, "Not too bad."

Her friend Martin was a professional *gaijin tarento*, a foreigner who made a living being a foreigner—a buffoon who could never do anything right in Japanese society. He always bumped his head on the high ceilings, forgot to take off his shoes when he walked into a house, used his chopsticks like shovels-so he made a career out of it. Martin had been Inoguchi's English teacher before he got a gig on a game show, and he told Inoguchi to watch out for her, how she had some sort of mysterious power. It was not true. The truth was, the most dangerous thing about her was that she was purely herself. There wasn't anything mysterious about it, she was just in the right place at the right time. Things happened around her despite how she felt about it. As far as she was concerned, acting natural was still acting. So the Buddhist idea of killing the self, of total selflessness, appealed to her.

Two years after her arrival at Narita, she was asked to teach English composition at Waseda University. If she accepted, she would be the youngest on the faculty, the only foreign woman in the department. Knowing she was out of her league, that her Japanese students probably had a better handle on grammar and sentence structure than she ever would, she had tried to refuse, but that only made them ask her more fervently. No one refused a job there. Finally, so her friend who recommended her wouldn't lose face, she accepted. And her worst fears had come true. She had no business being there at all, walking swiftly down the hallowed halls from which would-be students committed suicide when they failed the entrance exams. She had thought those reports were exaggerated. Now she knew for sure. But still, she taught English like everyone else, attempted to pull the clam-like students out of their shells. She rarely succeeded, but she tried her best.

She told Inoguchi he was sure that if she'd had to take the same exams, she too would have taken a sword to her belly—if anyone did that anymore (they did not). Still, somehow she had gotten the job, been at the right place at the right time. She could just as easily end up on the street, a place she'd certainly been before.

Another truth was, everyone said it was going to be hard to be a foreign woman in Japan, but she hadn't found it that way at all, because she had met that hardness, countered its force with her own. Besides, she knew how to hide her strength and no one knew what to make of her so they gave her anything she wanted, if only to get rid of her. Many Japanese still thought all the *gaijin* in Japan were just bit actors in an incredibly complicated film. As far as she was concerned, she could play any part they wanted and never lose herself, because her self was not to be found in appearances.

They got down to it.

"You move well," she said, smiling her Mona Lisa smile.

Mona Lisa because this line, like all the others, was dumb and she knew it and he knew she knew it and there was nothing either of them could do about it but smile.

"I never danced so close to someone before."

"Dan-ced," she said slowly, with a hard accent on the n.

"Danced," he repeated. "Danced."

"Once more, go ahead..." she said encouragingly.

"I never danced so close to someone before," he said steadily, deliberately, an edge to his voice.

"Excellent. Do you like it?"

"It's perfect. It seems like something I've always done, ever since..."

"What?"

"I can't tell you. Yet."

"I'll be waiting," came the coy reply.

They read for a while, came to the part where they slept together. He still didn't know who the leading lady would be. A *gaijin* for sure, blonde, white, willowy. Maybe of a certain age, like him. Michelle Pfeiffer, or Melanie Griffith or Jessica Lange. What's her name—Meg Ryan. She would be good.

Had he ever kissed a foreign woman? She wondered. He was studying her lips as she sounded out the words. It was a kind of ritual, him looking at her lips moving slowly, she watching him watching her.

"What's wrong?"

"I feel so awful for what I have done. I should not have taken advantage of you like that. It is completely unforgivable. How can I make it up to you?" He said this last line painstakingly slowly.

She rocked back in her chair, folded her arms across her chest and wondered what he would say after he had made love to a woman—foreign or not.

"No... please..."

Suddenly, he broke character.

"Maybe in the Meiji era men talked like that. Maybe they even thought like that! My grandfather might even have said something like that. He might have even felt that way. But not me. How ridiculous," he scoffed at the script in front of them.

But she read on, trying to keep from laughing.

"What century are you from? I don't know how the women are where you come from, but around here it doesn't work like that anymore. I made my choice last night, just like you did. Don't be so chauvinistic."

Whoever was writing these scripts knew nothing about the Japanese, she agreed. It would probably be a big hit... Hell, many Japanese didn't even understand the Japanese. But who understood Americans, either? Fortunes were built on these misunderstandings.

"You think this is dumb, don't you?" he asked, putting his hands behind his head and stretching backwards, pushing gravity, feeling her eyes on him and liking the focus it gave him.

"Yeah, it's the worst script I've ever read."

And then when she laughed he laughed too, because she was honest and honesty was a valuable commodity in a world of appearances, and he liked it. Besides they both knew it was themselves they were reading about, and they mocked those shadows because they felt superior to the stock lines and awkward apologies. They thought they would both handle it differently.

"Better get them to change the script," he said, his eyes on hers just a bit too long.

"Let's go on," she said, meeting his gaze.

"I can't explain how I feel about you."

She looked down at the page, but the lines were not there. She looked up at him.

"Explain," she said.

"Explain," he repeated in an exact echo of her accent, tone and pitch, moving his mouth in perfect approximation of hers. She wondered when the film came out if he would sound like some radical Berkeley hippie or techno-punk co-ed, understated cynicism wreaking havoc with his proper *nihonjin* Japanese manners.

"Tell me if I'm doing it right." He went back to the script, enjoying himself

"You are," she said, playing right along with it.

He took a sip of his Perrier, cleared his throat and repeated the line that was not the line.

"Say it in a whisper," she said, and he did, brushing her leg lightly under the table with his knee.

"I can't explain how I feel about you."

Then he held his knee against hers. She opened her water, swigged it out of the bottle. She shifted in her chair, got some height and moved her legs.

"Is this what foreigners think Japanese people talk like?"
He hit the script with his fist.

"Some foreigners."

"Not you?"

"Don't think so. I don't know yet."

He had a two-year-old son. She was thinking about that.
She wondered if the boy had ever seen a foreigner, if he
would cry at the sight of her blue eyes.

"I'm not telling you everything. I can't tell you what's
going on yet. I guess I should just leave now. And we can
forget that anything ever happened between us."

Inoguchi put the script down.

"I need a break."

She said nothing, nodded and pushed the script aside and
leaned back in her chair. He leaned forward and she could
smell his clean clothes, neatly laundered and folded with care.
That smell comforted her because it was the smell of domes-
ticity and balance, something she'd not had too much experi-
ence with in life.

"Come to Okinawa with me," he said suddenly, looking
down.

"Okinawa?"

"Have you ever been?"

"No."

"I'm going next week. With Shizo Yamasuke."

"Yamasuke Shizo?" She couldn't believe it.

"Yes. We're doing a play. Come see it."

Shizo was the famous Kabuki actor, an *onnagata* female
impersonator whose portrayal of women was more feminine
and graceful than the real thing. It was said that Shizo captured the essence of femininity better than any other onnagata

in Kabuki history, and of course, better than a real woman herself.

She was interested, thought she could learn something from his distillations of walk, gait, gesture, expression. The more artificial you looked, the more real you seemed to others, she realized. The artifice was the art, the beauty of it, like a Japanese garden.

She had heard that Shizo made it seem as if he had entered the spirit of femininity and became it, transcended his own gender with that first strike of the otherworldly bamboo flutes and the curtain rising and the shouts from the third floor flooding the stage, Shizo! Shizo! Shizo!

"You can come down and check my English," he offered when she did not respond. She knew that he did not need her to come down to Okinawa to check his English.

"How long will you be there?"

"A week."

"I can't," she said automatically, then cursed her impetuousness. Of course she could. She could, and she would.

"You can see the show we are doing. We'll have dinner. You don't have to stay the week... Just one night."

"One night?"

"You can stay at the Imperial. Unless you have some objection..."

Objection? The truth was, she was totally free to do whatever she wanted with whoever she chose. She had been engaged to be married to a rising young professor, but one day she woke up and knew she did not want to be an "academic wife." She wondered what the point of all those words and books and plans was, when what was happening was outside the mind, in the body and the guts—all those places the modern world had covered up so coldly in circuitry and silicon and high-definition TV screens. She wanted to lose herself, remembering that someone once said "to be lost in Tokyo is better than to be found anywhere else" and she agreed. She wanted to be so totally lost that she didn't even know it. So one day she moved into an abandoned, dilapidated house, a house with two four-and-a-half *tatami* mat rooms downtown. The owner had probably died and left it to his children, who didn't tear it down because they couldn't afford the land taxes.

She moved in, mended the roof, scrubbed the floors. There was no bathroom so she went to the public bath. But she liked the public baths. You met people there. Old people. Young people. Modern citizens of an ancient city. Anyone.

What mattered was that she was on her own after six years and it was delicious, that freedom. This way, she could live within the circle of the Yamanote, the green train that ran around the city like a hyped-up snake. If she lived outside the line, in the landfill, she'd be stuck in packed commuter cars with stale-breathed *sararimen* who felt her up in the morning rush hour and feigned innocence as they looked into the centimeter of space between their bodies as if that distance alone would absolve them of any responsibility. But it did not. She feigned innocence too.

"The Imperial?" she asked. The rooms were at least four hundred dollars a night.

"Yes. And you can go back to Tokyo the next morning."

This last a statement that required only an acknowledgement. She wanted to say yes, but what was holding her back? Some ridiculous moral standard she'd never believed in but upheld because in her world it was morally better to be righteous and then talk about the temptation as something you had conquered, bettered...Yes, it was morally better to be right-eous, she thought, but it sure wasn't as interesting.

"But. Your wife..."

"My wife?" His eyes widened. "Oh, she will be coming down to join us after a few days. Of course, with my son."

"Of course," she said. "I'd like that."

"Me too," he said and smiled innocently. It was deceptive. It was like a Japanese bath that's been sitting for a while so that when you first get in the surface is hot and you think the rest will be too, but the water all around the center is cold.

"I will send you the ticket."

"Thank you."

"And if you'd like to go to the match, we can go see Owada beat that pretty boy."

"I'd like that too," she said.

She looked at his watch on the table. They still had an hour left. She took a breath.

"Okay, back to the script. From the top," she said.

They continued to read and stop, read and stop for the next hour, not looking up until the receptionist tapped the frosted glass door and brought them hot towels to wipe their hands and faces with before they left.

When they walked out into the street, she asked Inoguchi if he knew of Shimada Yuji, the actor who had jumped off the thirty-sixth floor. He said he didn't, so she told him the story.

"Every time I pass this building, I think of him. But I'm still here, looking at the building. That story reminds me to appreciate living," she said.

"Every city has its stories," he replied. "Just make sure yours ends well."

They said goodbye at the station, and when she walked home she let the rain fall down upon her and didn't feel a drop of it, not at all. It was then that she heard what the crow was saying: Now. Now. Now.

The next day the ticket to Okinawa came, and the day after that, she went to the southern island. Taking a taxi from the Naha airport, the taxi driver guessed that she was Russian. No one ever knew where she was from, and she liked it. He said he imported vodka, but only drank Japanese sake. Didn't want to pollute his tastebuds.

At the hotel's lobby in Okinawa, a woman in a gilded kimono played the koto on a raised platform, her head bowed in concentration. The music's sharp twangs made her feel something of the primitive, something of what the Japanese islands had once been.

Inoguchi was waiting in the lounge drinking orange juice from a brandy snifter. Rehearsal would begin soon.

★   ★   ★

The play was about a woman who had fallen in love with two men—one a frail intellectual, one a heartless, virile brute. Together they made the perfect man. The story was an old one, better told by Dostoyevski, yet she looked forward to its retelling.

When the evening's performance began, the audience rose to its feet and cheered the actors, as if at the Kabuki. Inoguchi threw her a kiss from the stage. All through the performance, a fly circled the air above the actors, buzzing loudly. The brute murdered the woman in a jealous rage on the eve of her wedding to the intellectual, then he spit in the face of his rival to soil him. Shizo played both the woman and the intellectual, both in white. Inoguchi played the brute, dressed in black tunic and richly polished leather boots. He even donned a beard for the part.

After the play ended and the crowd had cleared she went backstage to congratulate Inoguchi. He kissed her hand. She smelled the leather of his boots. She saw the photograph of his wife and child on his dressing table, and he noticed her looking at them, but nothing was said. They were taken by limousine to dinner, where they had seafood dishes she had never seen before, small fluid sculptures on the black and gold lacquer ware plates. She had so much sake she could barely stand. Shizo's attendants were in waiting, all young boys with thin muscular arms and high laughter. They laughed, and covered their mouths like women when they did it. They danced and sang together, and she enjoyed it, felt fully alive. After all, she was among actors. They were all actors, herself included, only some got paid better than others for doing it.

After dinner they took the limo back to the hotel. Inoguchi walked her to her room, and they stood outside her door for a while.

"So how do you feel about me?" she asked.

"Like a little sister. Someone I want to take care of," he said.

"The position is open," she said. "Be my guest." She'd never had an older brother. Now was as good a time as any to adopt one.

She unlocked the door and went in. He did not follow. All night long she thought about the evening, decided what he wanted from her had not been English lessons, but had not

quite been sex either. She laughed to think that it was he who
had been pure and she who had been otherwise, at least in
mind.

In the morning, she went to his suite for the lesson.
When she knocked on his door and he opened it, she could
see his script on the desk among a pile of books and newspa-
pers in his room. He also had various cookware assembled in
the bathroom—rice cooker and a daikon radish grater, among
others, because he refused to pay the high prices the hotel
charged when he could cook it just as well, if not better, himself. His parents had run a small country ryokan, after all, and
he had helped with the preparations. The more she knew
about him, the more she had begun to like him in earnest.

He took out his script and put it on the formica table.
She took out hers too. He then took out his watch and placed
it face up on the table next to the script. He opened his
mouth to speak, and what came out was not English. It was
not Japanese either. They both burst into laughter.

"I'll never really learn English," he said.

"And I'll never really learn Japanese," she replied.

"But you know what? It doesn't really matter. We understand each other just fine. Maybe better without a common
language...." They looked at each other and continued to
laugh, because he too, now, was being honest.

"Better get them to change the script," he laughed.

"Impossible. This is the way they like it," she replied.

So he began to read, slowly and perfectly. She listened to
him, glancing at the morning paper, open to the sports page,
on his table.

"Once more," she said, and he complied.

She was surprised to see that Owada had withdrawn from

the fight because he had sprained his wrist during training. She wondered: What kind of fighter sprained his wrist before the big fight? A real one, she decided, or a dishonest one. Someone human, prone to mistakes as often as triumphs. Or someone beholden to others. She wanted to know which one.

Inoguchi saw her looking at the paper.

"Oh. Owada again. The bets are off."

"Yeah, it's a shame. I wanted to see him fight," she said.

Actually, she had wanted to meet Owada from the beginning. She told Inoguchi this. He smiled knowingly, as if he had seen it coming. Then Inoguchi said he had told Owada about her too, and that he would arrange everything.

And so it was set. Inoguchi would be the matchmaker. They would meet back in Tokyo. Somewhere in Shinjuku; they would find a place. Another drama would begin.

This time, she decided, she'd make up her part as she went along. And it would end well, it would.

Reply to Anything

D^{ear} Yuriko:

I'm wearing a pair of socks my younger sister gave me. They're very comfortable. Dark blue. She gave them to me over twenty years ago, but I have worn them less than a dozen times. I only wear them when I want comfort or when I want to think of home and what it felt like to be there.

She and I are different.

I remember walking on the street with her. She was like air to me. We didn't pay any attention to each other, but it worked well for us.

Take care,
K.

★   ★   ★

I had come to expect these thin sheets of paper in a hasty hand, each time mailed from a different town. For twenty years it has been like this, and I had come to look upon them as news from another country, one I had once lived in and longed to return to, a country that never really existed. A country called Japan.

Had he been lying? I asked myself this daily. It was difficult for me to believe him, that he had loved me, really loved
me, all those years.

And still, over the years, I had fallen in love with K at a
distance, where it was safe. Where no one would ever know.

Each time I opened my door and knelt down to pick up
the envelope from where it had fallen between shoes in the
genkan, I thought how most people considered us lucky to
have survived; how lucky we were to live in a time of peace
in a country of void where we could feel no loss. No loss!
Each time I received word from K., not being able to send a
reply was loss. All I could give was through my life, the simple actions of living, those he had given up long ago, those
whose devotions in his name he'd never learn.

★   ★   ★

I am in the habit of leaving the phone off the hook.
Now, someone else has called but the call has not gone
through, and it is playing a computerized version of "Lara's
Theme."

Sometimes, someone calls early in the morning after my
husband has left for work and the children are off to school.

I used to pick up the phone and ask in a gentle voice: Is
it you?

And then I'd wait. One breath, two, three.

I do not know who it is because they never spoke.

And yet, I could not help but think....

It is true what they said about what happened on the
mountain. I have never understood why. Because I never want-

ed to understand, for fear it would ruin my love for K. Because that is the nature of passion, and calling it into question only kills it.

I was thinking this, had come to this knowledge as if it were some obvious wisdom I'd purposefully overlooked most of my life, and the next letter I received from K. had something resembling an explanation. Even though he is somewhere undefinable, he knows me better than my own husband.

He never calls anymore and I wonder: Who has cut the line?

★   ★   ★

Getting older, I appreciate the difference between my sister and me. I have not seen my sister in many years, but the funny thing is to find people on the way whom I really feel are my sisters and brothers.

Sometimes they are my father or mother, or my uncle, or even my grandmother or grandfather.

But then, I am on the road again.

★   ★   ★

Did I flatter myself by noticing that he had omitted the word "wife?" Had he never found anyone, in all those years, who could be such a woman to him? And yet, the steady letters he wrote to me. Was I the only one?

There was nothing to be gained by being calm.

My house had grown dark, and my energy made the rooms seem frenetic, and I thought of K. and the way we had been back then. Us students, cloistered in old oak offices, quietly listening to him as he spoke, flicking his cigarette with his thumbnail to knock off the ash. Sometimes he stood in front of us and spoke with his dark, wild eyes.

What more was there to do?

K. didn't believe in miracles. Neither did we.

We had gone there, ruddy-cheeked and victorious with the idea of change, not because we believed in them either, but because we believed in K. Believed him anywhere: in the dark coffeeshops where he would read Eluard, and sometimes Rimbaud, who, at sixteen, had known more than many would know in their entire lives. We too believed we could be "Mixed up in politics. Saved." Only with K. as our guide. And then, giving myself to him for the first time, and ravenous at any chance to have each other, that was how it began.

But when the trouble started, K. had fled. Left everything.

The students would say they sympathized with our concerns, this said without stopping as we handed out our fliers in the courtyard. How I hated those words, which never led to any action!

And I would take the lead from K., stuffing folders into their hands anyway, talking with them as they walked, ashamed, though when I walked home from university my own hands were mild and my arms vaguely hung by my side like impostors uncertain of the success of their disguise. I was such an impressionable girl. I hated my parents, my youth, my country, my life. I wanted to be different. Not passive. A revolutionary.

★   ★   ★

At night, I pull the small book from under my pillow. As my husband sleeps quietly next to me, I read the words K. once read to me, words of Rimbaud, his favorite poet:

> Still but a child, I admired the intractable convict on whom the prison doors are always closing; I sought out the inns and rooming houses he might have consecrated by his passing: with his idea I saw the blue sky, and labor flowering the country; in cities I sensed his doom...

After K. disappeared I waited for five years for him to come back. I did not care what had happened in the past. His passion let me forgive him everything. Then, suddenly I gave up. Shortly after that I married. Soon I had children of my own. They say I was a good mother. Yet when the work was done it was K. who occupied my thoughts. Except that when I think of K. it is in the way one thinks of tragedy at the other end of a big city. There were days when I would watch the movie "Hiroshima, Mon Amour," over and over again, because I wanted to be on the other side of town, having found something worth dying, or living, for.

There were days when I could feel him near, almost as if we were back at university, when we sat on an old leather couch that smelled of urine and cigarettes and talked of revolution. How seriously we pronounced the word! We'd jump when we were excited or furious at some injustice, imagined or otherwise. But we had come there furious. Not at the usual score of political or class injustices, but because it had all been strangely anonymous around us, everything that happened, and we wanted to name it. We wanted to name ourselves through the naming of it. Now K. does not even have the prison of a name. Only an initial, which few use or know.

Looking at my husband each week-end bearing a load of work in brown envelopes home and me scrambling to nurture him, I envied K. his freedom. Although he has written that he is imprisoned by his past, he travels like a silent river. As for me, I will always exist in my house, defined by my husband sitting at a small table surrounded by six *tatami* mats beneath us and four walls to the side, and our children to our sides.

That is why I keep K's letters in a box.

K—he knows the stars, the names of trees, has slept on a rock pillow. I will not romanticize his wandering. He has survived: outcast or outlaw. What was the difference? I read and recall, read and regret:

On highroads on winter nights, without roof, without clothes, without bread, a voice gripped my frozen heart: "Weakness or strength: why, for you it is strength. You do not know where you are going, nor why you are going; enter anywhere, reply to anything. They will no more kill you than if you were a corpse." In the morning I had a look so lost, a face so dead, that perhaps those whom I met did not see me.

Me, I have begun so many things! There is not a thing I would change about my past, except everything. So I concentrate on simple tasks. I become a housewife, invisible. Like all the others.

★   ★   ★

I talk with a friend. I confess that I have fallen in love with K. She says she falls in love all the time, and that it is a good thing, that fantasy is useful, a motivating factor.

"He is not a fantasy," I protest.

She cups her cup of tea, warm in her hands, and breathes in the steam, nodding gently.

I turn and leave silently. She feels sorry for me.

I ask another friend, a man.

He too says the same thing. He smiles condescendingly.

He went to a different university, but was part of things at that time. He says "Aha." That is all. He understands.

For women, he says, chaos and irrationality compete with structure and ordinariness and work. This is natural, he assures me. A fact of life one must accept.

"Only for women?" I ask.

"No, for everyone. Only women feel it more, because they feel things more in general, right?" He touches my hand softly. He wants to have an affair. I know, because he has asked me before. For a brief moment, I consider it. Then I push the thought away.

But how to balance the two? I wonder. How to achieve both in life? "It is not possible," I say, "To balance."

At this, he laughs. No, it is not possible.

Still, there is a kind of hope in his laughter, and I can't help but feel that he seems relieved to talk about it honestly. It is almost a friendly pleasure. A guilty pleasure, but a pleasure, nonetheless.

I know that there is some way, and that K. has chosen me to find it. What's possible is only a matter of thinking it so. Then acting on it.

"Reply to anything, but answer nothing. That is what I have learned in my travels," Rimbaud wrote one dark, wet night before he died.

*   *   *

This is what I remember: K. standing at the lectern at lunchtime in front of a group of students gathered in an empty classroom on campus. I can almost see how he would grab the air, as if grasping motion itself from the molecules, and how, during an earthquake that made the lamps sway and the windows rattle we would come closer together, pulled closer for the lack of escape that had brought us to him in the first place.

Those were the happiest moments of my life. Such a sentimental thought. Was I still such a child?

*   *   *

At night, in bed, I pull the letter from K. out from the book of poems under my pillow. The explanation of the murders:

The case of the United Red Army. It is, even now, a difficult issue to understand. There are a few interpretations in my mind. But the most valid one for me is the emotion of self hatred which ruled them. I say 'them' because I was never really a part of them.

Why did they have a camp in Haruma Mountain?

They wanted to remake themselves as strong, true, revolutionary soldiers. Strong, true soldiers. This meant to them: humans who would die for their idea of revolution and would never have the fulfillments of ordinary life. Furthermore, they did not make an allowance for the weakness of human nature. But it is impossible to remake living humans as machines of revolution, isn't it? Because everyone has some appetites and sometimes wants to complain.

And then, suddenly:
I want to see you.

★   ★   ★

I fall asleep with the letters on my lap.

The next morning my husband wakes up early and finds the letters fanned across my body. He picks one up, holds it, and places it back down against my chest. I wake up.

He says nothing.

I make my husband and children's lunchboxes with their favorite foods. They take them and leave to work, to school.

When everyone has gone, I get dressed and I make my way to Hibiya Station. It is lined with police. I feel a shiver in my spine. They are here not for me, I tell myself. After all, I am invisible. A common housewife bearing shopping bags and food for her children. Something has happened.

★   ★   ★

The Japanese New Left movement began to decline in the 1970s. Some of the members of the Japanese Red Army went to Palestine or North Korea, because they couldn't find the future of revolution in the Japanese public mind. The Japanese United Red Army was established by the remaining members of the Japanese Red Army and the New Left, who had become frustrated and isolated. And so, I think I cannot call the incident revolution.

I cannot even call it heroic. I can only call it the tragedy of mass self-hatred.

K. once sent this letter to the newspaper, and it was printed right after he escaped.

To me, he wrote:

I think now had it not been for my own selfishness that my sister would have stayed back, would not have gone to the mountain to look for me and joined us. I would not have killed her.

We tried not to recognize our weaknesses and appetites. We wanted to eradicate human feelings. So we must have hated ourselves, because we could not get rid of weakness or appetite from our minds. To be a true soldier meant to deny one's humanity. And when we discovered the weakness of our comrades, which was expressed unconsciously, the hatred we had turned toward ourselves individually became directed at each other.

That's why the murders began. It was a kind of insanity. She had come there only to find me. I loved my sister.

*   *   *

I scan the policemen lining the street, shifting and glancing around nervously. I recall the words from K.'s letter, after the explanation, an expression of regret.

Loneliness is something I feel often when I stop.

He had never said the word "stop" before. Something would happen. Something dramatic and implausible. I thought about it, probably to delay my return to the unglamorous ordinary woman I had become, and perhaps always really was.

I am walking, walking slowly on the overpass to the train station when I notice the crowds gathered, slowing, gazing, gaping. The overpass shakes from the weight of trucks on the freeway above, but no one seems to notice. From my vantage point on the corner of the walkway, I can see people emerging from the subway, mouths covered, staggering. A woman falls, clutching her purse. I see two hands on the red leather bag, unmoving. It turns to blood in my mind. One hand rests at the bottom of the strap, the other, frozen and clenched, grips the top. The hands are white and very very still. I don't look at the body, cannot tell if it is dead or alive, but I am unable to move, thinking of this person on their way home or perhaps just having left, frozen in some implacable gesture caught by hundreds of passing strangers. Gripping a purse.

I have been there before. No, I am still there. I have been frozen most of my life.

People push me to get a look, breathing heavily, coughing, some laughing nervously. I turn to look at the crowd: they are the only real spectacle, because the victims doesn't really exist.

And then, suddenly, police appear, and with the sound of sirens I think of K. What would I do if I saw him? He doesn't really exist anymore.

Then a fire truck comes, and there is shouting, and it is then that I notice people everywhere, and some strange smell in the air. A large metal pulley is laid on the street. Men in orange, the orange that convicts wear, surround the people. They sit on top of some of them and pump their chests. Others talk animatedly, debating what course of action to take.

My eyes are fixed on the women's hands. The hands that grip the purse strap. One bears a large gold watch.

They are not beautiful hands at all, and miraculously, they begin to move. Minutes later, the woman is pulled from the street. A stretcher is laid out on the street for her, but she refuses to lie down. She can stand. She can walk. She insists.

There is no blood. How lucky! People say. To think that she has had a blanket placed over her shoulders and that in this moment she can walk away while others have died, choking and sputtering.

To me, it is as if she sleepwalks, in shock, and it is I who has been injured in the drama, having wanted to be bigger than that, just once, bigger than life. Are we no different than the students of my youth, we who gather around and gape, wanting to belong?

As she raises her hand to brush her hair away from her face, the image of K's sister comes to me and just as suddenly disappears. I see a woman much like myself: a housewife in her forties, resigned. Because where K's sister had died in the bud of youth, this woman had lived. She had been on the verge of death but had been pulled back into life by a will stronger than hers. Or perhaps by her own will, unrecognized.

I turn my wrist away from my watch and put my hand back in my pocket, heading home.

Coins fall at my feet.

I reach down to pick them up, only they are not coins, but rather bits of the watch my father gave me.

Casing. Dial. Face. Ring. The inner workings of its mechanical heart. Exploded. I quietly pick up the pieces. For no reason, I begin to cry. What is this city we live in, where people choke and die on the street? What is this world I live in, saving letters from a fugitive in a box and dreaming of someone I don't even know anymore?

It is a watch my father bought in Switzerland when he was 21 and had just graduated from the university. It was his first trip abroad. He had travelled with his father. And he had bought this watch for his father, who had worn it until he died.

Then my grandmother wore the man's gold watch with the black crocodile band, green from age on its underbelly, until she too died. My father gave me the watch when I last went home.

I pick up my bags and walk away.

I have left my husband a note. I have asked my parents to take care of my children for the evening. I have put my affairs in order. No, they have always been in order. I have left them the way they have always been. Because the truth is, I am like air to my family.

Now perhaps they will notice me. They will notice me in my absence in a way they never had in my presence.

I throw the pieces of my watch in a garbage bin on the street, aware of a policeman's gaze. Suddenly, the group of policemen in gas masks turns the corner and walks away from me. I walk slowly along the street, lightly kicking the golden ginko leaves splattered across it. I find a small inn on an alley near the train station and check myself in for the night. It is five o'clock, and soon it will be time for dinner. What will my husband eat? What will my parents tell my children?

I will take a bath at the inn. Soak for a long time, eyes closed. After my bath I will have only a few hours until morning, when my breakfast will come at seven o'clock and I will have to return home once more. When I go home, my husband will want to talk about the letters. About K. About my past. I never told him about my involvement in the Student Movement during college. His family even checked my background before we got married, but somehow this information escaped their notice. I do not want to talk, to answer. I think of the scores of broken watches I have saved over the years, the letters from K in a box. When I go home

I will burn them. I will tell my husband everything. I will face my past, and my future.

I do not have much time. And yet, it is more time than I have ever had in my life, it seems, because up until now I have always borrowed my time from others.

The door slides open, and I am brought tea by the hotel's master. I sit down at the *kotatsu*[1] and fold the blanket over my lap, tucking my feet into its warm, comforting folds. I get out my pen and paper, and this is what I begin to write.

My reply.

[1]A Japanese table with foot-warmer and coverlet used in wintertime.

The School of Things

The gallery was in between exhibits. Late one night, the sculptor snuck in and began to set up his show. The gallery had no windows, but there was a skylight in the ceiling and on a clear night you could see the moon and the stars through the opaque slanted glass. The night the artist set up his sculptures, you could see seven lightly shining stars and the moon.

That is, you could see part of the moon, maybe the part that Copernicus had seen through his telescope or Michelangelo from one of his scaffold contraptions as he painted the Sistine Chapel. The artist left all the lights off so that no one would know he was there, and he worked in the dark. Setting up his exhibit, he thought of his father and the small moments that made up life. As soon as one thought came another was on its tail, a comet pulling him into twenty directions of the past.

That night, the sculptor didn't look out the skylight to see the moon and the stars or a vision of his father's spirit. He merely set up his sculptures in the blackness, feeling in the air like a navigator of darkness for what remained of the man he had lost. While he worked, scenes from the past surfaced, like the appearance of a small animal or patch of lichen that had attached itself to wood. He would listen to the memory playing itself out, and he would answer it by holding the odd wooden shapes in his hands and moving them from one place to another in the gallery. He had to drag the bigger pieces on the floor slowly and methodically, pivoting them around on their largest corners. The smaller pieces were like difficult, imperfect fragments of memory, and he had to arrange them several times before they would settle in place. When the sun came up in the morning, he would know he was done. Later that night his show would open, and he would move on.

Last year he had taken a train to the mountains of Aomori, returning to the home he had lived in as a child. The occasion was his father's funeral. On the way to the ceremony at the temple, he walked through the huge *wasabi* fields, their sharp smell rising around him and stinging his skin. Somewhere in the distance a small fire burned. He remembered taking his shoes off and letting the dirt and wetness of the wasabi fields seep through his toes as if they were growing there, too. As a child, he'd imagined the fields to be magic woods and had wanted to stay until nightfall. Now, at the funeral he pulled up several handfuls of roots and stuffed them into his pockets, leaving some dirt still under his fingernails as he walked toward the white lanterns of the procession.

At the funeral they chanted Buddhist sutras, the voices in uneven tones that didn't mingle. They burned the body and picked the bones out with long chopsticks, saving them for the gravesite or altar urns. For some reason, he kept one of his father's teeth, slipped it into his pocket. Afterwards he went back to his mother's house to drink sake with the family. He had gotten scrubbed up and clean, remembering then when his father had taken him to a Western symphony as a child. They had gone to the *sento*, public baths where they sat on the small wooden stools and scrubbed each other's backs and poured buckets of hot water over their shoulders to rinse the soap off before lowering themselves into the scalding tubs. He remembered the way his body expanded like a tea bag, and here, now in the gallery setting up these blocks of wood, he realized that it was the last time he had seen his father's naked body. He closed his eyes and tried to re-learn the lines and striations in his father's veins through the wood as if it were a globe to be traveled as he sculpted.

The sculptor had taught his own child the names of plants and the seven grasses of springtime, so that the things that had once seemed great mysteries of the universe were no longer distant and unobtainable. They had names his daughter could sing to her friends in the schoolyard or say to herself while walking home through the city streets, echoing above the din of cars honking and the bells of the train doors closing in the distance: lespedeza, patrinia, althea, eulalia. She could call these words out, names of exotic natural princesses, and he would have taught her something of his country.

The sculptor moved the wooden pieces from table to floor and when he worked he closed his eyes in the darkness, remembering not the perfume of the ladies who sat behind him in their velvet dresses imported from Paris or the minerals of the bath water still on his father's skin, but the dirt under his fingernails from planting morning glories in the window boxes in June, as he had done every year with his mother. *What will you keep of me when I leave this world?* his father had asked.

When his daughter was born ten years ago, he wasn't allowed in the hospital room with his wife, so he waited outside in the hard plastic chairs, side by side with his parents. His mother had shifted her legs and his father had fallen asleep, his head bobbing like an apple in water. They had said nothing to each other but when the nurse announced that they could go in, his father was the first to stand up and walk down the corridor to the ward, first to reach the metal bar around the bed. He remembered the way his father held his wife's pale hands, comforting her. He had been a weak child himself, but when he saw his daughter's body on his wife's chest, he knew they would be healthy. His father softly cried. The sculptor's wife was American, and he suspected his parents had never been too pleased about it. But a grandchild changed everything, brought love back to the family and opened it up again like a flower.

He remembered when the people had rustled the last of their programs and the tympani had sounded and the cellist ran his bow against his strings to test his tone and the clarinetist wet his reed on his tongue and he remembered when the man in the next seat's lumpy body began to droop in its chair and when the great crescendo of music enveloped him like a giant clap of thunder. Now he crouched on the gallery floor and closed his eyes, drifting into these sounds all around, each one a small animal from a wild forest somewhere distant but near. And then he thought: this is music too.

Sometimes his daughter came to him before she brushed her teeth and asked to be told a bedtime story. When nothing came to mind she asked him to picture something unusual and he would picture his wife and daughter in bed together, small round heads propped up against yellow pillows, each one with half of the book on their lap, sharing the story. They would take turns reading the pages, whispering stories of a boy who rode a giant turtle through the ocean or a dog who hated to take baths, or seven Chinese brothers who swallowed the sea whole. He told her of a boy who went to the zoo and set all the animals free, or the little girl who could fly. His stories were clumsy and arbitrary, but if his daughter minded she never said anything as long as he put in lots of colors to catch her mind's eye and told the stories in a way that made her forget about everything bad that had happened to her that day. He always did that. Yet, all of his sculptures were black.

He cut wood and burned it with fire and sometimes filled it with water, sometimes with earth. Some of the shapes were circles, others were long and heavy, many were blocks. Since his father's death, he worked in the dark. If someone would come in and see the artist moving his works they would turn the lights on, as if a mistake had been made or someone had overlooked the simple fact of a light switch.

At the opening, photographers would snap their cameras and critics' pencils would move across their pages. People would walk around the sculptures trying to understand them, but the sculptures would not speak, and the artist saw little reason to add anything to his work. Those who looked and listened would know all there was to know about him through these pieces of wood, as he himself had come to know when he was working.

Cutting wood with his father, he had once asked what the circles inside the wood meant and his father said that each circle was an age—maybe a hundred years or a thousand years—and that each circle got wider and wider as time went on, filling up the space inside. He remembered the way the leaves stuck to his father's boots and the snapping sound the twigs made when he stepped on them, but the forest silence was the strongest sound of all. That much he had learned in Aomori.

Somewhere there was a river that passed through the

mountain carrying small silver fish. The boy and his father would stop there to catch them until the stars would rise all around them. They would carry the *aji* home in a basket and his mother would cook the fish carefully over charcoal, sliding a stick through their silver-gray coruscant backs. She had taught the boy how to break their heads and press his chopsticks into their backs and slide the backbone out whole when he ate them. It hadn't been easy to do, but after many attempts he was able to extract the small bones and the vertebrae. Then he could eat.

As he set up the sculptures he wanted all these things to stay with him forever, but when the last piece was settled he would leave the gallery and wait. But the people pulled him into another world, the so-called real world, the very world he had created his sculptures to escape from in the first place. Many people would come and bring sake and weave themselves into the rows of potted flowers that lined the gallery walls. Those who didn't have invitations would gather at the door, trying to peek through it to catch a glimpse of the famous artist. He would be with them, pressed up against their coats, trying to see what they saw. They wouldn't recognize the man with dirt in his fingernails who stood outside in the cold beside them.

They would walk around the wood, scratching their heads, trying to classify him or his creations. They called his type of work "The School of Things." Yet they seemed to learn nothing from it. The sculptor would take off his shoes while the others would walk loudly in their leather shoes and ask questions they could not answer themselves. Some would offer theories, saying the shapes represented the everlasting cycle of birth and death, creation and destruction. Some of them would say they had no meaning, that they were vessels. Some of them would say anything, but the sculptures didn't speak.

Tonight, on the first anniversary of his father's passing, the sculptor realized his father had not taken him back to the wasabi fields of his childhood to tell him how the plants grew, or to talk about the names of the constellations, or to identify the animal cries they heard after dark. He realized, too, that his father had never seen his art. And yet he understood that one way or another, his father had taught him how to be an artist. That much he now knew, and he was glad to have had such a father to learn from in a quiet, almost invisible way.

So he stood in the dark and waited. When the last guest had gone and the room was empty again, he unwrapped his father's tooth from a silk satchel. He placed it deep within one of the hollowed-out sculptures, as if under a pillow, like his father had done with his own tooth when he was a boy. Then he said a wish for his father's happiness, as his father had once done too, and left the light on as he walked out of the room and gently closed the door. Later that night, after he had climbed into bed with his wife, his daughter came into the room, the pitter-patter of her feet awakening him from a dream.

"Daddy, daddy, tell me a story," she said, pulling on his sleepy arm.

And so he sat up in bed, telling her about the things of his childhood: the *wasabi* fields, the *ayu* from the river, and the seven lightly shining stars and the moon. Now they lived in a world of concrete and steel, but someday soon, he promised, he would take her to the mountains and rivers of his homeland and teach her what he had learned from them.

Ghost Stories

All of her foreign women friends were witches. That's what Yukihiro, her Japanese lover, said. She could hardly argue with him.

Was she a witch too? He wondered. He was a writer who lived alone in an old wooden house near the fish markets on a twisted street, and she was his first lover. He wrote love stories, but every time he tried to write about her the page stayed blank. He never finished anything he wrote.

The street had once been filled with such houses but was now lined with shining white mansions, huge lighthouses in the quiet neighborhood pond. She wondered what the street had looked like when all the houses had been like his, but when she watched the fishmongers in their thick rubber boots fill their tubs with water she could no more imagine the lives of the past than she could envision the deaths of the future.

She had never been with a Japanese before. Everything seemed new, mysterious, otherworldly. Except the fishmongers.

She watched the men catch the slick brown fish in their fists and hammer sharp nails through their heads and slice their bodies with thin steel knives, slicing them so quickly there was no time even for regret. She wanted to live like that, but then she had met Yukihiro.

—Little sister! the men called out to her sweetly in the morning when she passed, where are you going?

They knew. They knew because they talked to her softly

as if she were a mermaid with delicate ears, and when she answered, "Here and there" they nodded their heads deeply, not looking up from their work until she'd entered the gate to her lover's home.

Yukihiro was from a small village in the Ryuku islands and wore his hair in a ponytail and dressed in old silk kimonos and went out at night to collect bones from the fish-mongers to put on his veranda. Bones for the stray cats who came seeking shelter, came every night to his apartment while he wrote ghost stories.

The old man who'd lived in the house before him had been a taxidermist, and when he had died there was no one to inherit the two-hundred-year-old family house, no one to sweep the *tatami* mats and change the white paper in the *shoji* screens or get rid of the animals, their bellies sewn in perfect stitch. And then there were the stories. He never finished them, never finished anything he wrote.

Yukihiro loved the cold blue eyes of the stuffed animals, their skin soft but not warm, like a fish so expertly sliced into sushi that its heart still beat on the cut flesh: alive but not liv-ing. She had come to his country with nothing, and they had met in Ueno where she had gone to see the lotus flowers of Shinobazu pond in full bloom. Two months ago, he had stood beside her for a very long time taking pictures of the flowers. She could feel the eye of his camera on her but she looked at the white flowers in the still water and did not turn to him. Finally she began to walk away and he followed her, asking her what she thought the pond might look like when the flowers disappeared in the cold winter air. All she said was *hai-iro*, which sounded to him like "hero" in painstaking English but what she had really wanted to say was "gray."

That day, Yukihiro had taken her to the noodle shop on the edge of the park where Mori Ogai had written *Wild Geese* a hundred years before. There was a bicycle leaning against the shopfront, and in the middle of their meal it had fallen over with a clamor. She had jumped slightly but he pushed her back down with his hand. Then he invited her home.

The first thing she saw at his house were the birds high on the shelves with the books, looking down on the ripped white paper of the old *shoji* screens that wore their sharp tears like scars. Fox and eagle and sharp-toothed viper. Animals of prey, bewitching things. He always took them down.

The books in his room: English, Japanese, Russian, Czech.

She saw him all through the spring when the lotuses were in bloom, but they did not sleep together until a month after they had met. His confession: he had masturbated to the pictures he had taken of her in Ueno Park, and the first time he had her legs tangled in his he feared he could not love the real her. Her confession: she knew he could, and would.

She wanted him to make love to her and not the image he had captured of her. *Without fail*, he said in the way Japanese sometimes do, *without fail*. I will learn to love you, he said. But when she stayed at his house he slept all day and apologized. She took the books down from the shelf. He had written down famous phrases in the margins of the complicated philosophical novels and moral quandaries that made up his thoughts but not his dilemmas. She did not know if he understood the other languages, or if the books were dead to him too, and she almost gave up hope.

Virtue is its own reward and *We can no more guarantee the continuance of our passions than that of our lives,* he had scribbled.

She did not know if he understood the words and she stared at them for a long time while he slept. When he awoke, she closed the books and could not help but think that the words he had scribbled were meant for her. But then again, Yukihiro was a modern man and a superstitious one at that, so he had left the animals where the old man had placed them, and she made sure to put the books back in the shelves the same way she had found them.

He could read English perfectly but could not speak it at all, his tongue having been meant for better sport. When they kissed it told her of the stray cats like the story of the body to impress itself upon her with its human needs, come to the veranda. To be needed! To cry for milk and say, feed me!

She wondered what kind of life of the mind a man like that could have when he bit her nipples rapaciously and ate her diamond earrings as if the very spirit of the abandoned cat purred inside him and called out to be taken care of each time his lips met hers. Still, he could not love her, and this made her desire him all the more.

He told her the critics said all he ever wrote about was love, but she was to learn that he had no greater chance of writing about love than one of the stuffed animals had of suddenly springing to life.

He liked the fact that she lived on faith and had a certain nostalgia for the old days neither of them had known. *Natsukashii*, he said. Nostalgia. Longing. But he didn't really know her.

She liked the fact that some day he wanted to live in her country, and that he was afraid of the water but slept with a full glass by his bed just the same. It was not often she fell in love at all but soon she could think of no one but him, this man who lived alone among dead animals and old words like some bridled and beautiful aesthete.

He, who said he had never really known a woman, had held her with such passion she could not believe him and wondered why there was so much to be said and no way to say any of it, not a word. And yet she thought he understood each muscle speaking its own tongue silently in the night between them.

But he had not.

Finally, he was able to make love to her. He was insatiable and ferocious, and she thought he might break her. But she could not be broken by love. She had already been broken by love, and bone by bone, she had mended herself whole.

From, that point on, whenever she called him he was not home. He did not call her for many weeks, and and then, late one night he called her, telling her that a strange cat with a haunted face came to him like a refugee.

He named it after the god of drunken revelry. Dionysus. Drunk, was he when he had named it thus? Or did the stray cat who had crept onto his veranda and into his room represent some inimitable recklessness inside him clawing to be let out, or in.

Perhaps it was a modern incarnation of the *preta* in Buddhist hell, destined to wander at the gates of its fiery inferno for a scrap of food, drink, love. No, it was just a stray cat, she decided. He was the one in hell and he would draw her down into it and she would go, willingly. Still, he would not see her. He said he could not see her any more, so she crept into his house and took the books out, one by one, when he went out on his daily walks to photograph the small crooked streets.

She discovered that he had put a green stuffed toy beside the cat, a soft round figure, a Japanese comic-book character, a senseless thing. She imagined that the cat loved the toy and had returned to it every night, meeting its false warmth with true affection.

Then one day he noticed his books had disappeared and he put Dionysus in the whoosh and whirl of his washing machine, turning and spinning underwater while he sat on his bed and held the blue sheets in a ball in his fist and laughed at his perfect cruelty. The he placed Dionysus on the shelf with the others, a still life, memento mori of all he had failed in.

Then he sat and waited for her to steal into his house. When she did, he grabbed her and slammed her up against the books and made love to her fiercely, holding her up against the bookshelves, her legs wrapped around his slender waist. When they were both satisfied she sat next to him and asked him to hold her, but he would not. Instead, he told her what he had done to the cat, pointing up to its lifeless figure on the shelf.

She asked: Had the cat known the rounded soft features of its lover to be inhuman? Was it wrong to love something that could not return your love? No. She knew that its crime was to have given witness to a love the man himself did not have—even if that love were no more real than the women he imagined making love to in the videos he carried home in silver aluminum bags at night, after work.

He said he could not believe that such beautiful women would act in pornographic films. She said she could not believe such a beautiful man would watch them, and she asked him to watch them with her and let her see what he saw. But he did not.

She supposed that in his school days he had studied the animal world: genus, species, etc. As for her, she and her classmates had pinned animals alive to small corkboards and cut open their flesh and peered inside the small yellow veins at the thin sacs of muscle and heart to see what made them work.

He said he sometimes played tricks on those he loved.

Forgive me, said the man who had once loved the cruel blue eyes of the stuffed animals. *Please*, he said softly, *you are foreign, and I am Japanese...* As if the difference were greater than that of books and animals, which could not be together.

Did you not know that before? she asked. *Did you think I would become Japanese?*

It can't be helped. For him, that was enough to say.

She went swimming in the cold blue water to wash him from her skin. She felt herself disappearing in the water, but then she heard his moans like music in her ears and suddenly the waves she made pulled her deeper and deeper into the knowledge that he had lured her to him only to abandon her on this strange island, like Theseus leaving Ariadne on Naxos. Surfacing, she noticed for the first time the three bruised finger marks on her thigh like a paw print where he had picked her up from the couch and carried her to the wrinkled blue sheets of the bed where they would stay all night but would not sleep.

She tried to forget about him, but she could not.

One night she dreamt that Dionysus came to her door, his fur wet and matted like muddy hay. She dreamt that she poured him some milk and when he drank it his tongue scraped against the bowl like sandpaper, and she was surprised to find that she had quickly grown to love him. She, who had always hated cats. She took him in, and from then on, he became hers in her dreams.

Soon it was December and the winds blew in, sweeping up sand and the stench of fish from the market and drawing her back to the park where the lotus flowers were dying and the impossibly thick leaves had turned into themselves, turned gray.

She gathered some in her hands and walked to Yukihiro's house, her feet burning into the ground like an arsonist's torch to dry wood. All of the stray cats in the city seemed to follow her through the twisted streets in search of a scrap of food, drink, love. But like her, they found none.

When she got to the old wooden gate she knocked, then pounded on the door but he did not answer. She knocked and knocked but there was no sound of life, so she broke into the house which was empty. There on the shelf were the photographs he had taken of her. She held them in her hands as if they were images of a dead girl in a happy moment never to be retrieved, and then she let them fall to the ground.

Yukihiro had been right, she was a witch, a dryad, and now she would return to that element, to the water from which she had been born, no time even for regret.

Leaving, she passed the fishmongers'. She waited until their backs were turned to step one foot after the other into the tub of water, looking into the sharp light of the gray blade that would soon be held above her in the fishmonger's steady hand. She turned into an eel and the blade fell upon her as sharp as Yukihiro's stabbing into her, and then she disappeared.

Yukihiro came home to find the photographs on the floor. He went to the lotus pond to find her, but all he could see was the still, murky water. He stayed at the park until nightfall wondering what it felt like to be needed! To cry for milk and say, feed me! He knew he had lost her forever, so he stopped at the fishmongers' on the way home and picked up some bones for the cats. When he got home he tried to write a story on the piece of newspaper the day's scraps had been wrapped in. But he could not. He knew that the pictures were looking up at him. He knew she had gone back to the country she had come from and he missed her, thinking only of her flesh against his and wanting her more than he had ever wanted anything in his life.

He walked out into the night and looked out for voyage in the light of the huge white mansions that lined his street like lighthouses in the quite neighborhood pond, but there was nowhere to go after all. Soon after that, he returned to the Ryukus and married his childhood sweetheart, but every time they made love he thought of the American. When he was with his wife, he had to pull away from her and run to his study to write.

From then on, he wrote only ghost stories. And he wished he could tell the American; he finished them all.

As for her, she would bury his unborn child and tie a red apron around a small stone Jizo statue in its memory.

Over time, the apron would fade like all the others.

Figures of Speech

A *word...*

What about the 63-year-old woman who had jumped off the six-story building in downtown Tokyo? On the way down, her arm had been caught in the fourth-floor fire escape, her leg on the third. Her right leg, her left arm had been severed. Something about the story made me wonder—something about the fact that she had chosen a six-story building to jump from—had she really wanted to die? Or was it just a remnant of a fight she had had with her husband on a fairly humdrum morning, prelude to a routine bad day, some momentary anger over which she would have forgiven herself the next morning, had she lived to see it. When that arm, that leg had been severed, she had probably felt an unbearable streak of pain, and like the Vietnam veterans, the ones in wheelchairs I saw on the streets back home, she had given up more than she had bargained for. More than any of us had bargained for. She never could have been whole again.

is sufficient...

The problem of what to do with a dead dolphin was something he hadn't considered in its germinal phase. He wondered if somehow Pierrot wasn't really dead, that maybe he was alive in some other way, some animal afterlife of which science had no knowledge. At the Aquarium he had watched the crane lift Pierrot out of the water and onto the stretcher, where the dolphin lay motionless for a moment until suddenly he arched like a boomerang and snapped into the air, his body convulsing in a spiral down the slick blue tiles of the Aquarium's floor.

to the wise...

She teaches English at a local private school. Sometimes she goes through the day's lesson without speaking, telling a student to pick up this stone, move it to the right, yes that's correct, now place this book here, this pencil here, like that. Nodding and pointing, she uses only the force of the gesture.

as a flick of the whip...

Syntax. Tonality. Intonation. As if each dolphin has a signature whistle, a frequency that constitutes its own language. Dolphins map out certain areas by emitting frequencies, then building a frequency echo in their brains so that the next time they are near that location, they know where they are. He thought the closest humans could get to this level of perception would be to walk, and to avoid physical objects in the dark: the low coffee table, the refrigerator, the dog's water bowl on the floor. The things that were bumped into until the fact of their existence was understood. He thought of Pierrot, swimming in his tank, agonized by the tiles that confined him, crashing into his paramours, Betty and Kim, breaking their bones with the force of his impact.

to a fine horse.

She walks the street, playing "duck, duck, goose" in her mind. She loves to pat children's heads; they are so soft and malleable, and the look of surprise and delight it elicits is icing on the cake. It's always the parents with their grapefruit eyes that squint and glare in sour reprimand, failing to see the humor in it all.

With your mouth and lips...

She had been asked for spare change fifteen times today. Just palm, look, nod. If I give a dime to each, she thinks, that will be roughly $1.50 a day. Enumerations of 10-cent vaccinations and 20-cent bowls of rice from countless orange UNICEF tins she had held on Halloween came back to her, floating above like some imponderable algebraic equation. It is regular now, this asking for change. At first, they were reticent to ask money of a foreigner. At first. Now they smile and let her coins drop into their palms.

closed.

He remembered the game "Operation" from his childhood. Faced with the representation of a man on an operating table, he would go into the body with tweezers and remove the bones, one by one. If he hit a nerve by accident, it made a loud buzz. Was there some way you could pick out bad thoughts from the brain without the alarm going off? Or were they determined to announce themselves, breaking and snapping obstinately. He had asked this of a man on the avenue, a man who caught fireflies in the air. "Always empty," he responded, laughing, and opening his palms.

how would you...

In German there are eleven different ways to say "to clean" but only two ways to express affection or liking for someone. In Japanese, the women's language does not contain cursing words. I wondered if language shapes a personality, can silence unshape it? Or was there something else, a form behind the silence, a sign offering meaning.

say it?

The dolphins starved because their food had been cut in the wrong angles. When the feeders went on strike no one knew how to cut the food correctly. The dolphins didn't recognize the shape of their food and refused to eat it.

I would ask...

She thinks of her housemother, wondering how many cups of tea she has served in her lifetime. How many times would her housemother have wanted to be served, to sit with her company and talk, unconcerned with how hot the small cups were, how tepid the tea, how fragrant the brew? Or would it make her uncomfortable?

you to...

The people on the street: a stream of colors, smells, sounds, movements, signatures. A girl in a white sweat shirt with a thin belt loop sewn between her shoulder blades stopped to ask him the time. What string had she hung by, this parachutist without a zipline? He imagined people hanging from all of the belt straps, chains, and cords they wore. People with belt loops on their backs, superfluous ties, buckles, snaps. Nothing connected. Suspended in air. Fireflies.

say it.

In his lunchbox, a puzzle: sliced egg, a pair of chopsticks splitting the center like an arrow, kiwi garnished with mint, cucumber, a small fish, ceremonial for the summertime. A sign of something. Good luck. Prosperity. Love. It was as if everything could be taken apart and put back together again. He pulled the thick hemp cord back around the box, and set it down on the pavement. Someone would eat it.

Have you asked...

There is a Japanese legend that if anyone who is sick can fold 1,000 cranes, they will return to health. A young girl with leukemia had folded 400 cranes and died, leaving her friends to finish the task. She had been buried with the cranes, like an empress buried with her dolls. I felt as if there were 1,000 cranes hanging in my head, wind screaming through their wings.

the question...

The clinking pachinko games, the faces strung like balloons bobbing across the bustling streets. The sing-song of this language, impenetrable. *Pachin, pachin, pachin.* She did not know how to say good-bye to her housemother who had taught her *origami* and how to wrap things, as if this, itself, would seal the future. She keeps the words under her tongue like a steel marble stuck in the slick striations of the *pachinko* path.

with your mouth and lips closed?

The shadow of a man had imprinted itself on the stairs of Sumitomo bank when the atomic bomb hit Hiroshima. He thought of this as he watched thousands of little boats floating down the river, symbolizing the dead's voyage down the sea. They glittered on the water, sails-out like the wings of a butterfly. He thought, too, about the three dolphins, and how they had starved for weeks. Sensing death, the snapper had begun to nibble at their tails.

Do you...

"When a woman leaves home in Japan," her housemother had told her, "she wears white, the color of mourning. She is dead to her family." Families sometimes built funeral pyres around their houses, to symbolize purification after the passing of the dead. She looked into the river and saw her face go up in flames, her hair sizzling.

have them...

Lanterns hung from the rooftops like the feet of ghosts, here the white petals of cherry blossoms had scattered on the ground, here scrolls of poetry lay tightly in their boxes, here the green crickets were fed melon rind. The rush of *geta*, the clattering of old-style wooden clogs. This I knew as the deliberate, hurried sound of women rushing home from market. How I hated this sound. I wanted to bump into one of these women, to watch the eggs, seaweed, sake, tumble to the ground, the woman's arms flailing in the air, trying to catch some of the products as they fell. I wanted to make the woman late for her husband, make the husband wait. A woman had gone to her husband's company picnic. Her watch had stopped so that she failed to prepare his lunch at exactly 11:00 when the other wives were setting out their husband's meals. At 11:30, she returned to the picnic with her child, with whom she had been playing. She had found the food spread out by the other wives, her husband's place empty, waiting. She had so humiliated him that she ran home and hanged herself.

or...

Pierrot did not die from starvation. The necropsy showed that his adrenal cortex had ruptured the day Betty and Kim had died. He lasted two weeks more, the sound of his whistle echoing in the empty tank.

not?

He thought about Pierrot as the escalator carried him down to the subway. He boarded the train and reached out for the plastic ring hanging by the strap, starting at the sound of his name. He looked for the sound: nothing but slaps of polished grey tile.

People began to open the pages of huge comic books, or novels with paper covers, or roll magazines to fan the wind on their faces. He watched the landscape unravel. The simple squares of rice paddies framed the field workers, their hunched backs and triangle hats superfluous. How were they inside, and yet still outside, uninterested or unable to look out from their own bubbles, or notice the trains jammed with commuters passing before them? He heard the jingling of a beggar's cup. He let the men in suits and hats rattle against him like the beads of an abacus, and he thought of questions and their answers, sometimes destined to collide.

(Author's Note: The italicized text in this story is gratefully excerpted from a Zen koan on language given by the monks of Tofukuji Temple in Kyoto, Japan, 1987.)

Thirty-Six Views of
The Imperial Wedding:
(A Small Fable in Homage to
Donald Barthelme)

1. Most of them had never seen a Hokusai, and few had ever seen Mt. Fuji.

2. Some of them had caught a glimpse of the Emperor, larger than life on the screens of their high-density TVs.

3. It was a question of degrees. How deeply could you disappear in the fog on any given day?

4. The imperial palace was at the center of the city of Tokyo. Therefore, there was no center.

5. The rest of the city consisted of tall buildings at 90-degree angles. Surprisingly, no one tried to climb them.

6. The buildings were all mirrored glass. This was odd for a country that covered mirrors in delicate silk hoods to prevent the sighting of ghosts.

7. Then there was the Crown Prince. He had studied abroad and liked the outdoors and was getting older and had no prospects for marriage.

8. And the Emperor, of course: what to make of him? And his wife Michiko, who wrote *tanka* and had nervous breakdowns and stared off into space like a ghost.

9. The Empress eventually disappeared from view. The press tore her to bits and scattered her like the petals of cherry blossoms.

10. Everyone was heartened by the fact that, after a long search, the Crown Prince finally chose a bride.

11. But then this new girl, a mere commoner, was *kowaii*. Scary. She had a career in diplomacy, which would come in handy. She was beautiful. She was brilliant. She could even pitch a baseball.

12. Anyway, the important thing is: He called and asked her to marry him.

13. Rumor had it that she turned him down. (The Japanese never say no!)

14. He asked again, just to show he was a man of his word.

15. She said no again. Maybe she didn't really mean it.

16. He had been drunk when he called, after all.

17. Everyone was drunk. Some of the time. So just to make sure...

18. They went duck hunting. The Imperial Household Agency intervened. There were threats made. The press broke the story of the impending nuptials. They were reprimanded for jumping the gun, and forced to retract the story.

19. The rest of us rode around the city on the green train. We learned about the engagement on our way to work, watching the small TV screens on the trains a few days later.

20. Everyone shopped for new clothes. You could tell by the bags they held in their laps on the subway, which were never allowed to touch the dirty ground.

21. Who says America's the only country that gets to have a strong First Lady? the editorials proclaimed.

22. When the engagement was announced, the press was cheered by the news.

23. Finally, the world had caught up to them.

24. He offered her a theory. He was a writer who wrote a famous book about pornographers. He didn't watch much TV anymore, and he didn't write much, either. He liked to drink and knocked over his glass as he talked. He wore sandals. His toes were pink and chafed and his toenails grew gnarled like the twisted branches of bonsai trees. His

wife and two daughters were part of a theater troupe where the women dressed up like men and imitated James Dean.

25. His theory: "Ever since we lost the war, you don't see Japanese men on television commercials.... The ideal man's a *gaijin*. An outsider. A foreigner. Women too. Japanese don't exist anymore, even in their own country."

26. All this talk about the center of the city being empty.

27. She was a Japanese feminist literary critic. She had a theory. "All Japanese men are looking for their mothers. Except that it's not their mothers they're looking for. It's the Emperor."

28. Most disagreed with both of these theories. Not that they said so, exactly. Because this was Japan, a country of "harmony and consensus."

29. They focussed on the Crown Princess. She was surpassingly Japanese. She was exquisitely modern. No one knew what to make of her. The truth was, she wasn't even a virgin.

30. But after a few years it became clear: they couldn't make babies. Would there be no heir? She suffered nervous breakdowns and disappeared from view. The press started to salivate, especially after what had happened in Britain.

31. The Imperial Watchers were left with nothing but outlines. If you judge a life by its outlines you get outlines.

32. As for Hokusai, there are more of his prints abroad than on the Japanese islands. If the perspective is warped, it could be a result of this trade imbalance.

33. Prints or prince: There is something wrong with always blaming it on the translation.

34. There are as many Japans as they are Americas. The nearer we seem to get to the one, the farther away we are from the many.

35. The only haiku Basho ever wrote about Mt. Fuji was on not being able to see it through the mist.

36. ...

Lighthouses in the Pond

Mariko came to me like a refugee and brought me their shoes, two by two. No sooner had my *noren* swung open than her hand darted in to offer up their shoes like a mother bird securing a worm for her baby. Some were too worn-down to save. Their hardened heels spoke of the men who had worn them so she pulled out the tongues and threw them away. She was taking part of their souls, and that's what she had wanted. But the good shoes, she asked me to save. Each week, she came with more. She said she would know, eventually, what to do with them.

She lived alone, or as she preferred to say, "by herself," in an old wooden house near the fish markets. Her mother had died shortly after she had married, and she and her husband, a taxidermist, had inherited the two-hundred-year-old family house. But now her husband too was dead, and all of his prized animals were positioned in various points in her home: atop the small refrigerator, hanging from the rafters, high on the bookshelves. But the moose, the wondrous stuffed moosehead was relegated to living room where it reigned over a defunct firepit covered with years of soot. Seeing it, those who came to visit would realize she was not alone.

Before the men arrived, she hadn't had a visitor in years—though she often extended invitations which were, by and large, ignored. She had visions of her husband coming to comfort her, repeating softly the words he had said on their wedding day, a sunny April Sunday so many years ago. *"Jusqu'a la mort, toujours l'amour,"* she would hear him say at night when the street had put head to pillow. It was something he had read in a book of French verse popular at the time of their wedding. It was a time when anything German or French was apropos, and she remembered those words, even now, though she had long forgotten their meaning. A university girl had once told her what they had meant, and she had never really noticed how much the words sounded alike until after he had left her. And then, for awhile, she had thought about death and love. But now she thought only of the men, and how to get rid of them, and how to keep her house and all the memories it contained.

At first, she welcomed the visitors, making them tea and rice cakes, chatting about this or that. But I had seen their sleek black cars pulling up to her house, and I had seen the way the driver nervously straightened the blue denim doilies and puffed out the white pillows the agents had been sitting on. I had seen the worried looks on their faces when they filed out of the house and made their way to their cars in the middle of the night. And I had seen the whites of their socks glowing as they padded towards their cars. And I had known they weren't happy.

Mariko, however, was never frightened by the appearance of the ghost of her husband. Rather, she was pleased to have his company and hear the echo of his laughter. It was much more pleasant than the men, always banging on her door and throwing stones through her windows whenever she so much as sneezed. And sneeze she did, for there were cats to be found in her home, abandoned cats, prone to periods of loneliness wherein they would howl and hiss, scratch and tear at the *tatami* mats. But she didn't mind them at all. They were just like her. And the men would bang away until she would be forced to pick up all of the cats and throw them out at the men, one by one, hoping to chase the men away, once and for all.

It was December, and very cold out when the cats stopped coming, one by one, and she was worried. The winds blew in from the waters, sweeping up sand and the stench of fish from the market. The other neighbors had gone on vacation, leaving her all alone in her house, sloping down into the concrete with each rumbling of the ground, as if her house were a foot bound by the earth's shoe which was too small to contain it. She had read that the animal world was cued in to certain dangers, and believed her cats were blessed with a similar awareness. But she had never put stock in what she couldn't see, and if she couldn't see danger, there was no need to plan against it. Besides, the men were short and had tightly drawn faces and when they talked their tongues scraped against their mouths like sandpaper, and she mostly ignored them, and they left without a sound. And each time it was the same. So she stopped answering the door. And they pounded at the windows and called her incessantly on the telephone. She pulled the cords out of the wall, and didn't leave her house except to hand me their shoes in secrecy.

Mariko hadn't been out of the house in days, and her stomach started to growl, and she cursed at the men, purely from force of habit, only to realize that the sound was emanating from her very own body. She was indeed feeling something, that rather unfamiliar pang of hunger, or perhaps it was loneliness, or even desire. It was a feeling she had felt from time to time, and had confided in the moose that the spirits of the abandoned cats were embodied in her belly. The moose, being wise and weary, looked silently at her, and laughed when her back was turned. I brought her food and company until winter was over.

Soon the sun shone through the frost. Suddenly it felt very much like April—it could have been the pleasant Sunday so many years ago when her husband had sworn he would never leave her. Only she knew it wasn't true. She felt something follow her as she moved slowly across the house, followed by a single streak of muted sunlight. It was the shadow of her past, the coming of the end of life. And she walked into the bathroom and stood in front of her broken mirror, where the face of her youth passed before her like a dream.

She ran a brush through her long gray hair, remembering her honeymoon on the Izu Peninsula, when her hair was black, as black as night. All the young men at the seaside had taken to lying on their mats, awaiting the moment when she would remove her robe, useless garment that it was, and reveal her daring swimsuit, always a shock of red. She made small jokes with them while her husband beamed at his new wife. They had all made quite a production of it. Holding hands, the young boys diving two by two gracefully into the salt water, racing underneath until they could no longer stand it, bursting to the surface, gasping for breath. She, older than they, swam out, out, into the slick green canvas of the water, breaking its surface like an eel until she felt the warm green waters turn cold and she knew she had reached the other side. She would raise her long arms above her head in triumph, squint her eyes and surge out of the water. All the young men clapped wildly and her husband smiled forever in the distance as she swam toward his open arms.

Their "good-bye's" were always full of promises to write, but the ink of such promises was invisible, and all such people that she had met flew in different directions like tiny birds.

She thought how easy it had been for her to pass through the water, knowing a future would be on the other side. Memory does not pass away so easily, she thought, wiping the stream of days-old mascara from the valley of her cheek. She studied the spot of black water on her fingertip and laughed to think how things repeat themselves. She found herself drifting quite often into places and times so long ago and far away that she had trouble locating herself now in her house, all alone. She told me these things, and I would listen and wonder what would happen to her husband's ashes and his animals, and her potted plants with delicate eggshells lining their rims like jewels.

A small good-luck charm hung from her window, reflecting kaleidoscope colors on the peeling walls. There was the ringing of a distant bell, followed by the cry of "*Imo! Yaki imo!*" from a sweet-potato vendor on the street. Slipping on her smock and old silk slippers, she shuffled about the attic collecting coins from jars and bowls, stuffing them into her pockets like a beggar. She bowed to the moose as she left, telling him she would be returning. If he'd watch for the cats, she'd most appreciate it.

Mariko revolved around the potato-cart like a cuckoo in an old Swiss clock, picking up once slice after the other, squeezing and smelling each as she went by. The potatoes seemed so old and rotten and she said so. The vendor laughed at her ritual and called her foolish—for she seldom bought anything, though she often invited him in for tea. Call me "Gen," he said, promising to visit when the weather was bet-

ter, but she just looked at him and smiled, grabbing the bag
of sweet potatoes he gave her. She heard the wheels of the
cart clacking against the street, the cries of the vendor becom-
ing whispers, melting, melting away as she walked slowly up
the crooked street to her house, where all the others once had
been.

She was eighty-nine, and she still tended the pots of
hydrangeas that lined the walkway to her house. She still
swept up the dead bugs and cut back the browning stems, and
still she pushed her hands into the rich earth and remembered
to water each pot, prune each flower. Construction workers
passed her and marched straight into her house as if it were
already theirs. They set up their land surveyors and measured
the plot of land, nodding their weightless heads as they dug
and measured, dug and measured. She tried to ignore them,
tending to her row of plants as if there was nothing else on
earth. The noise from the jackhammers swooped down on her
like a hundred vultures, but she pruned away until she brushed
her hands upon her apron, signifying the fact that she was satisfied.

Sometimes she'd describe the way one soiled his white
suit by bending beneath the floorboards, insistent upon finding
his new Italian loafers. Still others would increase their threats,
sending their drivers down the crooked alley in search of
cheap slippers that weren't too young or too feminine. She
laughed when they returned with plastic bathroom shoes decorated with flowers or talking kittens. She began to take pleasure in the way their faces blushed up scarlet when they realized that the woman had not gotten up to fix them tea at all,
but rather had scrambled into the other room to make their
shoes disappear forever.

At first she felt sorry for them, then anger would come into her throat like a wave and she'd say it was what they deserved. Hadn't she wanted them to feel, even momentarily, how she had felt? Hadn't she wanted them to think how it felt when someone took something that was yours, rightfully and inscrutably yours, without so much as an apology? And all the memories of the quiet little street stood by her side. All the wooden houses lined with potted plants, the sound of green onions being chopped against wooden boards in the morning for *miso* soup, the *futons* being shaken out and beaten from the balconies. The music of that. The wooden gates and sliding doors and busybody neighbors and the potato seller pulling his cart down the street. Now he had a record, and it wasn't even his voice that echoed in the alley. True, he too had gotten old, and singing aloud like he used to was impossible. But still, she missed the cracks in his voice, the cracks in his cart, and the friends she had known. Now, all of that was gone. Hers was the last wooden house remaining on the street, the others torn down and replaced by shining white "mansions" that seemed like huge lighthouses in a quiet pond.

After she had refused their hundredth offer, she handed me a rolled-up scroll and told me to hide it. It was the deed to her house. She held it like a sutra, and I hid it without words. She never saw it again, and I too, forgot where I had put it when the men came knocking at my door and demanded to have it. Even then, she believed that people were basically good, and that man's only real desire was to satisfy himself with the least possible exertion. And she wouldn't give in to the men who would tear her down like a memory. And she fought. And I fought with her.

First there was the cold water that had stopped mid-shower, sending the scalding water into her skin like fire. Then, her heat had jammed in wintertime and her gas reading was higher suddenly in one month than it had been her entire lifetime. There were warnings from roach exterminators, fires set under her house. There was the team of land surveyors who assured her monthly that without a doubt her house would not survive so much as a minor earthquake, and that she'd do well to take their settlement and live out her days elsewhere. She had ignored them all.

There was a small police box at the end of the alley, with a plaque outside registering the number of city-wide injuries and deaths. Each day the number stayed the same. It always read 0. I took her to complain about the men and their threats, but since my neighbor had no direct evidence of bodily harm, no charges could be brought. When we protested, the policemen were unmoving: hadn't they knocked, after all, and hadn't she let them in, welcomed them, and served them tea, even? She clucked her tongue and nodded her head. He gave us a basket of raspberries and sent us on our way.

I remember the way she took the berries out of the bag and stared at them longingly. They were red, deep burgundy red, as her lips had once been. The heavy cream we bought smelled sweet and comforting. She arranged the berries neatly in a glass bowl and spilled the cream over them like waves, watching it swim into the open spaces. She held it high above her head as she walked, schiff-schiff, on the hard wooden floor, settling into a pool of sunshine.

Mariko lifted the small spoon to her lips, swirling berries around in her mouth in a balloon of cream. She turned to tell me her husband was sitting snugly on the *tatami*, holding his hand before him like a gift. She found herself surrounded by the young men at the seaside, still dripping with water, but before she could welcome them, they became a mere puddle of water upon the floor. She held the bowl of cream to her mouth, feeling its soft warmth on her lips. The liquid swam down her throat, and when she swallowed the cream, she swallowed with it every drop of loneliness she had ever felt. She said that the spirits of the abandoned cats were purring inside her belly as she walked toward her husband, reaching out to kiss him for the entire world to see. But the world saw nothing. She said she saw the moose look down, and that she heard him laugh a wise and weary laugh. When I left, she asked me to keep an eye out for the cats, should they too decide to come visit. She never saw them again.

*   *   *

A few moons have past since then. Sometimes, at night, I think I hear Mariko singing. But it might be the wind, or the waves from the sea come up to town, or the ghost of her dead husband, or the spirits of the abandoned cats.

As for the men's shoes, before she disappeared, she took them to the post office and sent them to Armenia, where there had been a terrible earthquake, and people were once again beginning to trust the earth they walked upon.

Sayonara, Tokyo

Jack Hayashi said that mine was a life lived with brio. It was bad timing for such praise. He said it the day I planned to commit suicide.

I was in the subway station when the earth shook and my heel—that fraction of an inch I had taken to be an ally—had failed me, miserably, inexorably.

He had been behind me, like a shadow. Maybe he had called out my name, or the name he thought was mine. Maybe he had asked me the time, always a common ploy. When I fell, I remembered a story and the color of his shoes and the way his pants had filled up with water from the puddle on the subway floor. And the time.

Such was the nature of desire. I was this close to the edge of the platform.

The story was this: Once there was a nun who wanted to devote her life to the study of Buddhism. She walked for years on mountain trails so that her feet bled, so that she cried out and made the wolves laugh. But when she reached the monastery, the humorless monks turned her away because she was too beautiful and did not belong where life was full of arduous tasks.

She left the compound dejected, this woman who could not know the monks were blasting kernels of barley in pots of water in their kitchen or spilling eggs on the carp who swam in their sacred ponds.

I tried to remember how the story ended. I was never very good with endings.

He pressed his fingers to my lips and held me to quell the shaking. I bit him because I had learned that this was an action a man would remember, one that would call to him in an odd moment. He would not remember the way my crumpled form had been resurrected on the subway or that the curve of my back asked only for a definition against his body, but this: the blood coming down like a flood of memories.

In the story, the nun tried again. This time, when she walked back up the mountain trail the monastery was quiet, several monks reposing on flat wooden beds, some of them locked in small dark rooms bobbing their heads like apples in water. She knocked softly on the door. When there was no answer she sat and waited until the rains came and they were obliged to let her in.

Suddenly, I remembered him. Berkeley High, 1984. Star athlete, the kind I always avoided, not for dislike but from fear of rejection. Classic. A wrestler or football player. Japanese-American guy I'd avoided as too different. Me, the skinny kid with the strange friends and a wandering eye. He, the kind of boy with a million friends and designs on no one special. The kind whose father had been an Air Force Officer in Vietnam and proud of it. 86th Airborne, something like that. Proud of it still. The kind who had probably changed now, become a bleeding-heart liberal who was drawn to awkward girls like me. The kind who probably now read Lacan and was always slightly vexed. In other words, a romantic.

There was the way he had picked up my shoe, so gently, as if it were a fallen eyelash. When an eyelash fell I placed it in the web between my thumb and forefinger and blew it off, making a wish. My morning's wish had been for love. And when it banged gently at my heart like a mosquito at a screen door, I let it bang. After all, I didn't even remember his name. I could already feel my face in his tumbling chest, his fingers in my hair. And no one else had ducked for cover. We were spectacle, strangers in each other's arms. I re-thought my plans for the future.

Surely, suddenly it dawned on me like the sun rising over Mt. Fuji—it was Jack. We had met before. But now again, in Tokyo. What were the odds of that?

"Berkeley High, remember?" I asked, looking at him askance. Then he noticed my shoes. They were on the platform, pointed together in prayer, the way a jumper takes them off before saying good-bye to the world.

"O-mi-god," he said. It was not without eloquence.

"My heel broke..." I lied. I had wanted to be an anthropologist so that I could go to distant shores, or a madman so I could disappear. Like Jim Morrison. Elvis. Benny Goodman. Like Dante in the mind. Instead, I'd stayed on the ground, forgotten everything good sense had taught me. To relinquish control. To trust my body to the other, to be passive, aloof, resigned. But I had enjoyed it, the defeat. I had enjoyed the unexpected frailty of it. I had enjoyed it so much I had held my fingers rolled into each other, tightened in small implacable balls to keep me from laughing out loud. I ended up in Tokyo, where one went to disappear. To reinvent oneself, to get lost in *pachinko* and broken English and broken hearts and money if you could find it.

Sometimes I went down to the tough dance clubs near the fish market and found men to dance with there. But when the earth shook that day in Tokyo, I had planned no strategy.

And there he was.

Just like in a fairy tale.

We went to a "love hotel", got our triangular key, unlocked the door, and that was it.

He asked me how I felt about double suicides. Did I remember the self-immolation at Sproul Plaza? Did my parents protest the involvement? How long had I thought of doing it myself? I told him there had never been any self-immolation at Berkeley. Only draft-card burnings and tear gas. I was adamant that he had romanticized everything. He was adamant that I had forgotten. I told him I'd come here to forget.

His father had done it, he said. Jumped in front of a train. It was tragic and messy and scarred him for life. His mother was so shamed they moved to America. He wasn't Japanese-American. He was *real*. His name was not Jack. It was Shinsuke. Amidst these confessions, outside a voice called out from a tin box in a policeman's chase, pull over to the right. Who are you and what in the hell are you doing here? Jack-Shinsuke wanted to know. I asked him the same thing. He was working for Hitachi, but in his mind, he was living in the 19th century, riding a horse over a misty mountain pass to meet his lady, sipping steaming green tea in the snow. It's serendipity we would meet like this. It's fate. I would marry you in a minute if you want, he said. After we made love. Of course, he said those things. I didn't believe him. Would you? He didn't even know me. That was always the best time to propose. I reached for my clothes. I put my pants on, then my socks. Lastly, the shoes. I had to get out of Tokyo.

We'd rented the room by the hour and the hour was up.

"We can pay for another hour. You said I could stay," he said flatly, smoking a Hope cigarette. It was as if he had copied his life after an Antonioni film.

I remembered the shoes. I got as far as the right one.

He reached for the left one. He pulled it away from me.

"Wait!" he said, "I will love you! I will speak your wonder to the marigolds and breathe your pain to the crabgrass that invades the earth. I will split your heart open and blow its tendrils to the mountain ranges like the seeds of a dandelion. They will fly to the West where the sun never sets and the potatoes never weep for lack of eyes! And I'll always wash your back when you bathe!"

It was like a bad translation of something in his heart. And it didn't sound like my idea of fun. Except the last part, maybe. I told him I liked Sylvia Plath and Anne Sexton. Mishima and Dazai. I could put up with Kawabata in small doses. And we all know what happened to them.

"No more talk of suicide," he pleaded.

I pulled my shoe back away from him and stuffed it in my pocket. I closed the door behind me. He tried to follow me but tripped on his own legs—each one the leaf of a drunken pinwheel. In a shop window I saw a wooden toy where a man flips down a ladder, head over heels and over again.

I wanted to run. As long as I kept moving, I wouldn't fall off the ladder. My father's generation had climbed it. My grandfather's had built it. My generation, we just ran on it, up and down like hamsters in a perpetual Habitrail. Damned and enjambed. I had come to Tokyo to survive my life. It paid the rent on each day's passing. The bubble was floating high up in the sky and I was holding on to it, rising. Teaching English. Talking to bored housewives over ten-dollar cups of coffee that tasted like Truckstop Joe.

Jack Hayashi. He was green and black in my memory. Green was the color of envy, black was the color of his shoes.

The next day he was waiting for me, 5:15 at Otsuka station. We checked into a different hotel. One in Shinjuku. Over the bed was a chipped painting of Titian. A reproduction, of course. We stayed there Thursday and Friday. Which stretched into Saturday. Then Sunday, when we went to the flea market at the old temple in the rain, walked into stalls, inspecting Imari plates and faded old kimonos, the air thick with sandalwood incense.

"Didn't they want you to stay in America? Your parents, I mean. Didn't you have a real job?" he asked.

"Of course," I said. I had worked in conservation. Wasn't working in conservation as real as you could get? " I didn't have real parents. They were drunks. Never there. They hated America."

I wrote grants, fought for the snail darters, small fish living in a big river an even bigger development company wanted to dam. I told him the story.

"What exactly are you trying to say?" he mumbled.

"Haven't you heard of the spotted owl?" I asked. Things on the verge of extinction.

"Never mind. Let's do it again," he said, pulling me closer.

*   *   *

It went on like that for weeks. We tried every "love hotel" in Shinjuku 3-Chome. We sucked *yakitori* from little sticks and *sushi* from plastic boxes. But then he would turn beautiful when he reached down to pick up a cigarette that had fallen from someone else's pocket to the floor, because he found life in discards. Castaways. Rejects. I loved him. I hated him again. Love. Hate. Life. Death. Sex. Literature. It was good to be alive.

I took him behind doors that read "Private." He tried to be kind.

He bought me flowers. Bouquets of day lilies he held in his hands. We would stare at each other for ages, taking an inventory of imperfections. He told me I was a survivor, like him. Because we had escaped from Berkeley. Made it to the Secret Capital of the World relatively unscathed. Tokyo. And now it was time to leave. We had to get out alive. Bonnie and Clyde. Shooting up the cardboard salarymen and the pathetic fake geishas as we made our escape.

I ask you now: wouldn't you covet those words?

Was there anything else for me, really, more alive than him, this divining rod disguised as a man who had unearthed my passion? To think that he didn't trust women!

And that I distrusted men!

"I still like Jimi Hendrix," he admitted.

"...And I listen to Kurt Cobain," I confessed.

"We're fucked," he said. We were broken children, after all.

We went out dancing. I saw how he watched girls in their black leather skirts tight against their bodies, lips thick with moneycolor. No doubt, their families were intact. I tried to imagine one of them with a scar on her face, a scar that came from wanting something so badly it no longer mattered how you got it or how it came to you but only that it did, with a force or power instantly set in a triangle of flesh.

I saw wounds everywhere. He saw healing. There it was,

the old Yin-Yang.

We had a kitchen in our new hotel room. The latest model of everything. The seduction of gourmet. The most popular room there.

"Do you wish your father were still alive?" I asked, tearing open a little bag of radiccio and endive salad you could get pre-made at the grocers. There were purple and blue leaves incongruously called "greens," since they were the color of bruises. Blues.

"Sometimes," he said.

"Me too," I said. "I guess."

"I thought he was?" Jack-Shinsuke said.

"Yeah, but he drank so much I never saw him. I mean, he never saw me."

"We have noted that the process of seeing effects a series of reversals..." he quoted someone (was it Lacan?) kissing my neck. "...the result of which is to bind together the subject and the visual object in a series of shifting relationships."

That was the most I had gotten out of him all week.

"You're so full of shit," I said.

"We're going to get old, you know. We found each other once. Let's hold on while we can."

We drank cheap sake and ate at the Sushi-a-Go-Go, grabbing the plates from the conveyer belts. We made love on red velvet floors. Or curled up on the linoleum of the capsule bathroom. He told me his father had been passed over for a promotion when he decided to kill himself. He said his father could not cry. Then it was like that psychological joke where someone tells you not to think of a purple elephant, and of course you can't help but think of a purple elephant. When we moaned I thought of his father in pieces on the tracks, and of him thinking of it. What was he thinking?

"You stuck around longer than I thought," he said, grinning.

"The food was good," I said.

I went to a salaryman bar after midnight where crusty old men lined the chairs like day-old riceballs. I went back to the fish-market clubs and danced with the men in a circle around my purse. I placed it on the scuffed wooden floor, as if the tiny gold bag were a harvest to worship. And I, who could not feel I belonged because all the women who were thought to belong were envelopes of other people's desire, wanted to be desired.

I drank small cups of Japanese gin and made toasts to the ones who were left behind. I toasted the men in wheelchairs. I drank to the lepers, saluted those who were loved no more. I hailed the people who thought only of pain. I tasted the smoke from the men's stale cigarettes and watched them scratch at their skins until my eyes burned from watching. Where was Jack-Shinsuke now?

They said I had the "up for adoption" sign in my eyes.

Something in my eyes, the three-white eyes, was a sign, the old men said. They gathered around me like fireflies. There was a theory that if you could see three whites around your irises (two sides and bottom), you were out of sync with the universe. You would die an early, violent death. Like J.F. Kennedy and Marilyn, like Gandhi and Malcolm X—all three—white eyes. If only they had gotten in sync sooner! I wanted to believe they would still be alive, that we could see them age like Mick Jagger. I wanted to believe things no one else believed. That the good didn't have to die young. That I was good. That I could live even if I wasn't.

And then, I remembered the end of the story. The woman walked back down the mountain through a small village to a house with a roof made of straw sticks where someone was ironing clothes of white and blue indigo. The beautiful woman sat down by the lady who stood ironing and took tea and talked of smelling the fresh mountain lilies and listening to the song of the cicada. And when the lady wasn't looking she took the iron and pressed it against her cheek and kept it there until her skin was on fire and she fainted on the straw-matted floor.

I was curious of the stature of the ugly because no one wanted them. They had somehow gotten hold of a deeper understanding of life and this understanding spoke like an iron burn and said that everything good had already been created and everything bad could not be destroyed.

I went to the bathroom and looked in the mirror, looked at my eyes. Maybe it was best to be out of sync in a world that was basically disastrous. Perhaps that assured survival. I felt, suddenly, that I had reached a deeper understanding. I went home and fell asleep. When I woke up it was 5:15.

Soon I was running to the subway station, running down the stairs when it happened again. 5:17 and the earth shook. My heel—that fraction of an inch I had taken to be an ally—had saved me. I saw that now.

And there he was. Jack-Shinsuke. Behind me, like a shadow. Maybe he said he finally remembered me, who I was. Or that he didn't care. That he loved me anyway. I forgot the story of the nun. His bags were packed. So were mine. We were leaving Tokyo. Saying *sayonara*. We were going to be fine.

"Don't leave me," I said.

"Not a chance," he replied.

I took his hand and held it tightly so I wouldn't lose

him. After all, it was rush hour and impossible to know where so many people were going.

The Hatchback

Clear tears and black dresses, white handkerchiefs pressed to red cheeks—that's what one expects at a burial. There were none of those things to be found that day in Zushi, however, when the only thing falling was the rain, which came down in much needed sheets after a year-long drought. The dirt was so wet you could call it mud, and the workers were laughing as they dug their shovels into it and flung it out to pasture. They had come to bury a car.

It was a dark blue American 1971 Ford Pinto, the kind that had been recalled for some manufacturer's defect, a malfunction or miscalculation. Stripped of its insides, the motley rusted horse had stood naked on the hillside, ruining the Yamamoto's ocean view. What was this strange creature, an American car, doing on Japanese soil? A burnt-out chassis, no wheels, no steering wheel, no doors, just an empty frame. It hadn't been there when they bought their summer home. But now it would not go away.

The Yamamotos had been looking at it for over a year, trying to get their neighbor Sano-san to remove it. But he never answered when they knocked on his door. Hoping to avoid further conflict and thinking he wouldn't notice its absence, they hired the men to bury it instead. They'd tried, hadn't they? They'd knocked, they'd left pleasant notes suggesting they all take tea. When that hadn't worked, they'd delivered a basket full of stone fruits in the summer, and dried fruits in the winter. Now what would they do?

The rusted metal heap was an eyesore that ruined the natural beauty of their summerhouse in Zushi, invading the verdant
hills once dotted only with young bamboo sprouts and threaten-
ing to hijack the very blueness of the distant ocean itself.

But their neighbor didn't see it that way at all. He didn't
have many visitors, but he collected old metal the way others
collected orchids, snow domes or pets. On any given day,
another old washing machine, refrigerator, stove or heater
would just appear. And stay and stay and stay.

The Yamamotos had a city place, a *pied à tierre* in a sleek
Tokyo high-rise, a beautiful red-bricked building with beveled
glass windows overlooking the city. It was just a stone's throw
from the Four Seasons, where they often had breakfasts of dill
omelets with goat cheese and pancini, Russian tea with a slice
of lemon that came wrapped in white cheesecloth tied with a
thin blue satin ribbon. Then they worked off breakfast at the
Raquet Club and headed out to the country, where the ocean
breeze kept things cool. In the summer, that was their life.

They drove a sleek Jaguar, named after the fastest and
largest of jungle animals, drove it down the crowded express-
way out of the city, past Tokyo Bay and Yokohama harbor
where boats dotted the bay like confetti. They drove through
the sprawling suburbs with their huge apartment blocks, drove
past the rice paddies and factories, and breathed a sigh of
relief to be escaping the rat-race world. When they hit the
ocean breeze, they couldn't help but feel blessed with the spirit of the Gods who inhabited this land.

The Yamamotos worked hard for this comfort, though
they never expected to have it. They hadn't always been rich,
and still weren't really comfortable showing it.

They had bought the country house on a whim, one day when they had been hiking and picking blackberries on the coast, visiting friends. Having a summer home had long been the dream of Dr. Yamamoto, who'd grown up poor in the countryside of Gifu and had made do with the other kids, playing on the concrete playground down the block from the schoolhouse. Dr. Yamamoto built his private practice (nips & tucks, what the Westerners called "cosmetic reconstruction") in the flush Bubble Years, and had invested the money well when he still could.

And so, counting his blessings, he decided to buy a little cottage on the coast where the family could go to escape the humid Tokyo summers. He liked hiking and bird-watching and going swimming in the beautiful backyard pool and enjoying a glass of chilled Kirin beer as he rested his elbows on the ledge of the deck chair after swimming a few laps, looking out over the sea. That was living. His poor childhood seemed a lifetime ago. His own children had never known struggle. Everything had been fine until the Pinto had shown up. It was as out of place as an apple tree in a bamboo grove.

Dr. Yamamoto was flummoxed. It didn't happen often. The Yamamotos were a well-liked couple with an easygoing temperament. The Dr. had many friends from his practice, and his wife Mitsuko studied flower arrangement at the local community center on the week-ends and even started doing yoga at the gym, though her legs fell asleep when they were crossed and she didn't like to sweat. Did yoga make you sweat? She hadn't realized that would happen, but it made her skin glow and she felt good afterwards. Everyone said she looked ten years younger than her six decades. She was happy.

They had two children, a son and a daughter, who had

turned out well—a doctor and a lawyer. But the kids had moved away—they both lived far away from Tokyo and had started families of their own. The beach house in Zushi was a way for them to get together, to enjoy each other against the slow pace of the ocean tides, drawing in, pulling out.

But the Pinto was a problem. The more the Dr. thought about it, the more it bothered him. Something about this car disturbed him deeply, or perhaps it was the fact that their neighbor, who seemed to be unemployed and out of place in Zushi, blatantly ignored their attempts to communicate with him. The car itself was unsightly. It had been driven to death, and like Ichabod Crane's horse without a rider, it had somehow been left with a strange velocity and a haunted spirit. The first year, the Dr. just closed his eyes and tried to ignore the heap, but recently, it had kept him up at night. He grew more and more agitated, lost his concentration, couldn't relax, became irritated and snappy. The Pinto had overstayed its welcome. Something had to be done.

The Yamamotos had met their neighbor only once, and very briefly, when they had first bought the house. They had stopped by to make a courtesy call and introduce themselves, bringing over some freshly baked bean-cakes. The man, unshaven, hair unkempt, had stood at the screen door and nodded gruffly—was it a mockery of their city manners? The house was a mess inside as well (Mitsuko had peeked in), but since that mess was hidden, it didn't bother the Yamamotos. That had been over a year ago, and they had not seen him since. Sometimes the light of a TV would flash from the windows of the ramshackle house on the hill, blinking its eerie message as talking to the abandoned cars.

They had no other neighbors to speak of. They had

bought this house because it had been far away from the other summer homes, a bit removed from the week-end fray. There were a few other summer homes up on the hill, but they were not often used. Perhaps their owners were too busy with city life to bother to come up and relax.

The closest thing to another human was an aging movie star who lived in utter seclusion up the hill in an old wood cabin. The Yamamotos hadn't seen him in awhile, either. Rumor had it that he was writing an epic book of samurai tales. He would be of no help at all, and was equally uninterested in contact.

Dr. and Mrs. Yamamoto tried to talk to some of the locals when they ran into them at the market or filling up at the gas station, but no one seemed bothered by the car. In fact, no one else had even noticed it. One day—which happened to be the Dr.'s 65th birthday—after keeping watch on Sano's home to see if his TV was on, the Yamamotos knocked on the neighbor's door, trying to would appeal to his environmental instincts: Wouldn't all that rust and metal be bad for the earth? Or the water lines? What if some of the toxins from the rust got into the neighborhood well by accident? They could all be poisoned.

Sano-san did not answer. Obviously he was home, pretending not to hear. Or was he out at the bar? The TV was always on, so it really wasn't a good indicator. Maybe he was sleeping, Mitsuko suggested. Maybe he was deaf.

Dr. Yamamoto was even more irritated. He had a hunch that if he went into the small town and checked in at the bar called *Soudaisa* (Grandeur) that's where he would find his neighbor. They had a pool table there, he'd been told. Dr. Yamamoto had played pool a few times when he was in residency in America. It was in Brooklyn, in fact, and he'd had some fairly tough competition, so he felt fairly confident in his game. He put on some jeans and a flannel shirt, walked down the hill, went into the bar and laid a hundred yen on the formaldehyde rim of the table. His neighbor was playing another man who looked almost exactly like he did. Stringy hair, faded pants with dirt crusted around the bottom, and hiking boots. Cigarettes hung from the corners of their mouths.

The doctor offered them a smile and loosened his stick with the chalk square as his neighbor racked up the balls and broke them with a clack. Then it was his turn to play.

"Doozo," Dr. Yamamoto said, letting Sano break.

At first, Dr. Yamamoto thought he would let his neighbor win. But then Sano-san screwed up his face and rudely sucked in his breath, breaking Yamamoto's concentration just as he was lining up a shot. He felt that he was being bullied. Just like when he was a kid in Gifu, playing "The 47 Ronin" with the older kids who cheated and beat him up because he was poor and his father was a laborer and his mother couldn't read. Well, he would show them that things had changed. Against all odds, he had money. He had power. He could win.

They played three games and Yamamoto won two out of three. Maybe now the man would respect him. All the while, he kept looking for a way to ask about the Pinto, but somehow he couldn't broach the subject. When the third game was over, Sano just turned and walked away.

So nothing was settled. How could this problem be solved? That's when he and Mitsuko had delivered the gift baskets, tried to broach the subject with kindness. Nothing worked.

In the end, it was money that did the job.

Dr. Yamamoto paid some local day laborers seventy-five dollars to bury the car, and he paid his neighbor $2000.00 for the Pinto itself. The doctor considered it a charitable donation, a contribution to the well-being of the hillside, and to his family and guests who came to enjoy the ocean view. If he'd wanted to see junk, he would have stayed in the city. But the countryside was grand, and an unobstructed view of nature's great vast gift of the ocean was one of the last refuges for the city spirit. If he couldn't salvage the rainforest, at least he could save one little piece of the countryside.

He considered it a small price to pay and thought the matter was settled, but then, Sano wouldn't let them haul it away. So they had no choice but to bury the Pinto, give it back to the earth.

Dr. Yamamoto didn't feel so good about it. "*Sho ga nai*," Mitsuko said. They'd tried everything. It couldn't be helped.

The day the car was buried, the Yamamotos stayed out by their pool, watching the men do the job over the fence. The pool was nestled in a Japanese-style garden, exquisitely landscaped, with bonsai trees and miniature rock gardens and a waterfall that rushed down from the rocks to the pool. The bottom of the pool was a royal blue tile. Mrs. Yamamoto liked to look into the water as if it were a reflecting pool, it made her calm. She pruned her bonsai, even though they were already perfectly manicured.

The men lifted the car and then dug up the earth. It took four men three hours to do the job, but they seemed to enjoy it, laughing a lot as they worked. Yamamoto couldn't help but think they were laughing at him. In the back of his mind, he was furious. He was still a sucker, still getting bullied. When the men lifted the car, hundreds of earthworms squiggled, frantically looking for cover. Once hidden underneath it, now they were exposed. Ms. Yamamoto looked at them and turned away.

Afterwards, she invited the men in for cold barley tea and watermelon. They sipped thirstily, wiping their hands on their overalls before collecting their money. When they left, Dr. Yamamoto had a strong desire to invite his neighbor back to the bar to shoot a game of pool together He wanted to play a good game with the locals, a fair game as equals, but the rain fell steadily and he built a fire inside and curled up with a good book instead. There was a huge brown spot in the grassy hill where the car had been buried. It looked like a wound in the land.

That night, Mitsuko Yamamoto, who normally slept soundly, dreamed that another junked car, an old blue Toyota Celica, had suddenly appeared where the Pinto had been. She woke up in a sweat. She knew it was just a matter of time. Would her husband have to pay to have it removed? How much would they charge him? Why didn't he stand up to that neighbor, who was only trying to cheat them because he thought they were rich?

Mitsuko got out of bed at daybreak and watched the beautiful sunrise coming into view. As the sun rose over the sparkling blue water, she tried to forget her dream. But when she went to take her early morning swim, she was startled to see that there were dozens of dead earthworms at the bottom of the perfectly clear blue pool, unearthed from the burial and washed in with the rain.

The Tale of Genji: Or Glass in the Face (In Which a Girl's Love of Scars Sours)

With no warning whatsoever, Genji's face began to shine. It happened right before the wedding. No one knew that Genji had been in an accident in high school in Yokohama. His face had gone straight through the windshield. He was a character actor; what else could he be with a face like that? Scars right down the side of his face, and across his neck in a huge red cord. He played yakuza and samurai, grizzled warriors and heavy-hearted ronin in chambara movies. Even the make-up men had to admire the way part of his ear had been torn off at the top of the lobe. And that snake-like ripple on his cheek. That was an effect that couldn't be manufactured, even with the best pancake. He was perfect for swordfights.

Carolyn was planning her wedding for the spring. She'd been planning it for six months. It would be at the Rose Garden in Berkeley. The roses would be blooming, and the whole family would be there. She had been dating Genji for a while now and she'd never felt happier.

They were going to drive off into the happily ever after in a 1962 Cadillac convertible, poison-apple red with fins and white leather seats, just like the movies. Her friends, were going to throw rice and cheer, and some of them would try to hide our envy of the girl who had caught the bouquet.

Carolyn wanted to marry a Japanese man. She said she liked their respectful distance and quiet good manners. They treated her like a woman, and she wasn't ashamed to have them open the door for her. Besides, they gave her a wide berth to be herself. And that was priceless. She had dated another Japanese man for a while, a businessman who was studying English in San Francisco, but she didn't speak his language at all and he didn't speak much of hers and she soon got tired of hand signals and silence. Then he left the country. That's when she met Genji. His father was American, so he spoke English pretty well. He used to pump iron in Venice Beach and went by the nickname Medicine Man. Carolyn liked the name because she said his love had healed her in places she didn't even know she was broken. She was always gushing like that and embarrassing her friends, who didn't think much of Genji at all. Except for when he was on-screen. Then, he changed into a real hero, the best in the wise-guy lineup. And no one could understand his lines. They didn't have subtitles in yakuza movies. Beat Takeshi had recently started getting popular in America. His latest was a really violent movie that made *Goodfellas* look like something from Disney, and Genji had a pretty big role as a loyal sidekick who commits suicide rather than betray the Beat, so his stock had gone up.

They'd met a year before the wedding, auditioning for bit parts in a movie about fishermen and unions. Carolyn was going for the part of the ingenue, and Genji was going for the union buster with a reputation for violence. They said she looked too tough to be an ingenue, so she was hired to serve coffee. It was all fiction anyway. Unions weren't very popular in Japan.

Genji didn't remember any of the accident, except for waking up in the hospital bed and having to pee, flailing his arms and legs as if rising from some deep dark sea. He saw stars for weeks and had that glazed-over look that survivors get when they emerge from a wreck, only half-realizing that they're still alive. Then there was a moment of shock when the curtain comes up and they understand it's the same old world they might have gotten a ticket out of had things worked out differently. Things never did.

Until he met Carolyn.

Everything went to hell in a hand basket the day his face started to shine. At first it was just a little spot on his cheek, but then it turned sharp and glistened, and if he tilted his head in a certain way, like a plant leaning towards the sun, it reflected on his face and shot stripes of yellow and orange and red across his forehead like a pinwheel prism. A piece of shrapnel emerging from a soldier's body years after the war had been all but forgotten. A repressed memory surfacing at an unexpected moment.

Carolyn was alarmed, but didn't want to hurt his feelings so she didn't say anything. She knew that love was never an exact science, and truthfully, the glass intrigued her. The other truth about Carolyn was that she loved Genji for his scars. She liked guys whose faces had fallen in some way, because people who had suffered usually understood the value of happiness. Because they had seen the flip side. Her father had been killed in a plane crash. His face had suffered wildly. There was an open casket at his funeral. Her favorite uncle, too. He had a stroke that left half of his face dead. Sometimes Carolyn wondered why she had a penchant for scars. She thought it had to do with survival, but everyone on earth was a survivor. After her father died she had been sent to a foster home where her foster father had beat her with a brick. She ran away and lived on the street, where she had been a hooker standing on dark corners. Genji had been her customer. That's how it went.

Genji knew the minute he saw Carolyn that she was on the threshold of doing something big. He wanted her to leave her old life behind, like a too-slow shadow. He told her to quit hooking and asked her to marry him. He convinced her she had acting talent, and sure enough at her first audition, she got the job. Okay, it was to serve coffee, but at least she got the chance to be on the set, soaking it up. So far, she had served coffee on three films, and Genji had gotten parts in them all.

To make a long story short, things were great for a while. Genji and Carolyn got engaged. But then, there was this blonde girl who came onto the set—the one who did get the ingenue part—all legs and red lips and curiosity, and one day she walked right up to Genji and said, "What's that thing in your cheek?" and touched it. He let the glass come out on its own and it emerged the size of a quarter. He gave it to Carolyn. He kept forgetting to show up for his driving lessons. How could you drive off into the ever-after without a license?

When the shooting wrapped up, Genji ran off with the leggy blonde, saying this was what gangsters were supposed to do if they were worth their salt. Not that he had anything to prove. Carolyn didn't have the heart to tell him he was a movie gangster. He wouldn't have cared. In true tragic fashion, she let him go.

"You'll find someone better," her friends said. "You'll find yourself."

She soon lost interest in the Cadillac and the happily ever-after, gave up on acting and went back to the dark corners where no one could see her face. But after a while, something inside started to shine, and she emerged like a butterfly from a chrysalis, glistening and new. Now she works at a Japanese restaurant and watches Kurosawa movies with her friends and knows every one of Mifune's lines by heart. Now there was a real samurai actor.

As for Genji, he went back to Tokyo, where no one looked at him anyway.

Green Tea to Go

The first English word Ryo learned was "weight." It was an unusual word, especially given all the more common possibilities like "hello" "good-bye" or even "thank you," but Ryo had been an unusual boy. That's what his parents had told him, and before long, he began to believe it. He was often beaten up in school for being "different," and eventually decided it just might be true. Just how he was different, he didn't know, but one day he imagined he'd find out.

He turned to foreign languages, foreign things and eventually, people. One day his mother brought home a strange contraption and placed it on top of the large wooden table in the kitchen.

It was a big scale of the kind found in England, with a metal tray curved up slightly on the sides, and a round clock face on which numbers and corresponding lines were printed. It was as strange and wonderful as anything Ryo had ever seen—except for the huge English dictionary his father had given him for his seventh birthday—which was as strange and wonderful as anything Ryo had ever seen before that. Since both the scale and the large book were English, Ryo decided they should go together, in the way that strange and wonderful things belonged nowhere else but side by side.

He put the dictionary on the scale. The dictionary had far more weight than cheese (this was what Ryo imagined was weighed on the shiny metal tray in England) and the tray crashed down, fell off the table and clattered onto the floor.

Now thirty-two and fluent in English, he had told the story to a spirited British girl named Michelle, to whom it had seemed unbearably funny. And ironic, since he was now standing in front of the *hakariyasan*, a shop for scales, weights and measures, explaining the various strange-looking Japanese things and what they were used for to her. There were scales Michelle had never seen, like the huge *kujirajaka*—a measure for whales, or the small round trays made for balancing fish or vegetables. To her, they were as foreign as the scale Ryo had encountered in his mother's kitchen years before, and she could no more imagine weighing a whale than he could imagine weighing crumpets (what were those?) or even cheese (what was that? He never really liked cheese). They had discovered the shop on the way to visit Ryo's mother, who was in the hospital, dying of cancer.

A strange-looking scale in the window had caught Michelle's eye, and she had pulled on Ryo's hand and dragged him in. She would later confess that she was nervous and stalling for time, but even Ryo was amazed that such a shop still existed in Tokyo amidst the world of complicated electronics and computers of every shape and size, and he was happy to enter. The old-fashioned Japanese scale, like the abacus, was utilitarian and somehow human—showing every scratch and sign of life, even collapsing when the load was too heavy, and stubbornly hanging on until the mechanism broke. Still, one couldn't throw it away. You could not say that about much else in Tokyo, except for people. But even they seemed to push themselves to the limit. That's why there was the word *karoshi*. Kaput from overwork.

Ryo felt as if he had fallen out of time. And yet, this ancient shop belonged here, a marker of time past on the road of the twenty-first century, felt right in the midst of this fast-moving chaos. Behind the shop lay the Meguro River, which was really a small canal—one that Ryo's father remembered fishing in as a child. "Believe it or not, Tokyo used to be a beautiful city," Ryo said. "My father and I used to go hiking in Gotanda." He was always telling Michelle things like this, in part to give her a sense of his childhood, in part to tell her that the "new" Tokyo was strange for him, too. That he was a fish out of water, like her. "Hiking in Gotanda?" Michelle was incredulous. She could imagine hiking in Gotanda—now a tangle of electric wires and high-rise buildings—as readily as she could envision swimming in Tokyo Bay.

At the hospital, Ryo waited for a moment with his hand still on the door before going in. He looked at Michelle. She would not be prepared for what she saw, he knew, but then again, no one ever was. He looked at his watch. They would stay for half an hour, depending on his mother's condition. He wanted Michelle to have every chance to know his mother, he wanted it to go well. He was surprised when Michelle smiled bravely at him and put her hand on top of his on the door handle, pushing it open and bowing as she entered the hospital room.

"Will your parents like me, as a British person?" Michelle had asked.

"No, they will like you as Michelle," Ryo answered steadily.

"That's not what I mean. You know what I mean," she laughed.

"I love you, so they'll love you," Ryo laughed back and

gently kissed her on the back of her neck. "It's really that simple," he added.

She couldn't hide her surprise. He loved her. Already? "You are unusual for a Japanese man," she had said.

"Why do you say so?" He imagined she had not known other Japanese men intimately, but couldn't be sure. Not that he wanted to know.

"I thought Japanese were followers. Group-oriented people who blended in. You don't care what other people think of you."

"But I do care about what people think. It only looks like I don't." He knew he still had a long way to go before he really lived the life he wanted, which was away from Japan and its conventions. He also knew that those very things were inside him, part of him. Inescapable.

"You act on your feelings. I like that."

He felt she was giving him far too much credit. But then again, hadn't he asked her for her phone number when they had met at the Butoh dance performance at the warehouse? He hadn't even wanted to go. A friend of his had done the lighting, so he had to go. Each movement seemed to have taken minutes to complete. The twist of an ankle. The bending of a leg. It was excruciating. Then he saw Michelle in the crowd, and looked at her the rest of the performance. He couldn't stop looking at her messy hair, and her beautiful sea-green eyes. He hadn't seen anyone that genuine, in a long time. He felt he had known her forever. Maybe she had saved his life once. They had both been samurai who fought for besieged farmers in feudal Japan. His mind moved deeper into these possibilities, and when the performance ended he walked straight up to her. She had taken his name card and had given him hers. And hadn't he later called her at 2:00 am?

Now, in the hospital, his mother smiled weakly and held out her hand. Michelle took it, and his mother began to cry. At that moment, Ryo knew they would be together. Not in another lifetime. In this one.

★   ★   ★

The weight shop became one of their favorite places to go. It was a place that never changed, inside or out. In fact, they wondered if anyone ever bought anything there and how it survived. Ryo decided to buy something.

One day, there was a new scale, a Western scale from England, sitting amidst the bamboo poles. It was like the one from Ryo's youth, and made him remember his childhood. He was happy to be able to tell Michelle the story, and to laugh about it and hear her laugh too. But Michelle did not laugh. She had something else on her mind, he knew. She had not told Ryo about the letters she had gotten from her parents. With a Japanese man, she would be doomed to a life of servitude, living in a country of people one could never trust, let alone really get to know, they argued. Her father remembered the war, even though he was too young to have fought in it.

Her mother sent her clippings about *karoshi*—death from overwork—and the Narita Divorce Syndrome, where couples broke up at the airport on the way home from their honeymoons. Michelle was surprised that Ryo's parents had accepted her without any qualms at all. It was hers who opposed Ryo, and she was ashamed. All the old stereotypes, and it was her family who had them.

*   *   *

Ryo decided to use part of his year-end bonus to buy the old scale. He brought it to the apartment he now shared with Michelle on a back street in Nezu. They took turns weighing things. Each time he put something in the scale, he revealed a bit of himself. She did the same. It was as if they were playing Japanese *go*, weighing their moves and those of the opponent. But nothing seemed to surprise her, not even the arm band he had worn to show solidarity with the worker's union on May Day each year or the large junebugs he had collected over the years. He was curious by the array of things she produced too—Native American arrowheads, crystals for healing, a money clip her father had bought in Tuxla, Mexico, even a picture of her old boyfriend.

Over time, it became their altar—a neutral space. Michelle put one of the letters from her parents on it, and Ryo read it. He replaced it with a momiji maple leaf, in beautiful russet tones. Not long after that, Michelle put an airplane ticket to London on the scale. After two years in Japan, it was time to return home, she said. The longer she was away, the harder it was to go back, she explained. Living abroad was a game of diminishing returns. And he could always come visit. She was sure her parents would like Ryo once they got to know him. Ryo stared at the ticket. He wanted to take it and rip it up.

He stood up and walked away. He couldn't believe she would leave. And yet, he knew that she wouldn't be happy if she stayed. But when he thought about living in Tokyo without her, it didn't make any sense. He would be lost without her. He thought about her words, "You act on your feelings," and he knew she was wrong.

He knew he was a coward. Damn that scale, and damn that dictionary for making him think otherwise, even for a moment. That scale had been bad luck. He took it out to the trash on the day when "unburnable" items were picked up. When he went back to get it in a moment of remorse, it was gone. Probably picked up by a foreigner.

★   ★   ★

"Please cancel my tea group," his mother said suddenly, awakening from her sleep one day they visited. Ryo and Michelle had been sitting in the hospital room for twenty minutes, staring at each other. During that time, Ryo's sister and her seven-year old son had come. Michelle thought it was a good sign that Ryo's mother's mind was vivid, that the first thing she had remembered was that she was scheduled to teach the tea ceremony that coming Wednesday. She had kept the appointment in the hopes that she would be better. Still, the fact remained that she would not be able to make it. "Yes," Ryo answered quietly. "And please pick up some *ahnko*. Right now you can get it at a good price at the Seibu department store," she said, almost in a whisper, smoothing a few thin strips of hair against her forehead with the back of her hand. "I will," Ryo breathed deeply, staring past the tubes all over her body, hanging in the air like strips of seaweed.

They all said nothing as they walked out of the hospital and down to the subway. "*Anko*? " Ryo's nephew Takao asked, taking Ryo's hand. "Why did grandma want us to buy sweet bean paste?" Ryo turned to him and smiled, laughing. Michelle understood at once.

"Not *anko*, but *ahnko*. It's a big fish with an ugly face, a winter fish. The season is just starting. She remembered that, I guess." Takao looked at Michelle quizzically but didn't say anything, just nodded as if he had known this all along. They got on the train and rode it in silence. " It's very good in nabe soups," Ryo said suddenly to his nephew. "I want to try it," Takao said, swinging his sock-footed feet from the subway seat. His shoes lay neatly on the floor of the subway car.

When Ryo's sister and Takao got off the train, Ryo asked Michelle how she had known the two words. "I just guessed," she said. Ryo said that it was his father's favorite dish and that his mother used to make it for him all the time. "Now that dad has gone, I must be the one to make it." They went to the department store in the Ginza, where women in fancy kimonos swirled around them.

Once home, cutting the slippery fish, Ryo found a large metal hook in the *ahnko*'s mouth. He was lucky to have found it, he thought, or else someone could have gotten hurt. Suddenly, he laughed. Who would imagine finding a hook in a fish mouth bought at a fancy department store, or a scale shop in the middle of downtown Tokyo amidst the highrises, or even a British girl in a dark industrial warehouse full of Japanese? And that there were words that sounded alike but had totally different meanings, and that things which didn't seem to go together did.

Was he really who Michelle thought he was? Was that some more courageous part of himself, buried deep inside? If Michelle didn't stay in Tokyo, Ryo decided, he would go with her to London. He could work at a bookstore. He wanted to belong to something, even if it was to a bunch of other people who were also unusual, weird, or even foreign. He wanted to belong to her. He belonged with her. He knew. He could be exported, transplanted, and still keep his Japanese roots. But maybe they could grow wider and stronger. After all, even McDonalds had green tea to go.

The next day, Ryo left his job at the bookstore early, and went back to the department store, where he picked out a simple diamond ring. He invited Michelle over for dinner that night, and decided to cook his best British meal. He bought London Broil, new potatoes, Guinness beer, fresh parsley, and for desert, an imported raisin pudding. It was a joke, but one she would love. Like the time she made him fermented soybeans and raw egg over rice with seaweed strips for breakfast.

When Michelle came later that night, she was carrying a large plastic bag.

"It's amazing what you can find if you look hard enough," she said, placing the scale on the *tatami* mat. "People throw away the most wonderful things, don't you think?"

Ryo took the ring box out of his pocket. He put it on the scale.

"Not me," he replied.

As Michelle opened the box and slipped the ring on her finger, Ryo finally knew what it felt like to be "different," which he now understood was just another word for free.

Poste Restante:

(A novella)

Anna is en route to Banda Neira, a dot of land that has fallen like a chip of topaz in the vast blue streak of the Moluccan archipelago, and she is alone. She had not expected to make the trip by herself; she had never taken a vacation alone. She is to meet her friend Juliette, but Juliette is not there.

Juliette had chosen the Spice Islands for their very remoteness, and Anna was drawn in by the promise of newness and the smell of fresh nutmeg, mace, and cinnamon on everything. She imagined a topography of volcanic mountains and a crumbling post-colonial beach town she could paint in pastel colors from the shore. She wanted to hike in old forts, to eat spicy food, to leave work, and Tokyo behind.

But it was Golden Week, the one week of the year when the Japanese took holidays, and flights were over-booked—full of girls in giggling groups, or shy young lovers on their first trip together. Juliette had been living in Japan without a work permit, and left the country every three months to renew her tourist visa. It was due to expire again, so she had flown to Indonesia ahead of Anna, promising to meet at a small Bali inn with huts on stilts, chosen from the Lonely Planet guide. And the back-up plan was carefully drawn: if for some reason

Juliette wasn't there, Anna was to leave a note in the Poste Restante telling her where she was. They would find each other, and together they would head off to the Spice Islands and have a wonderful time. Except that is not what happens at all.

It is in Bali, deep in the smoky basement of the Den Passar post office, that Anna realizes Juliette is not coming.

She has been taken first to the beautiful inn, with its thatched-roof cottages and blooming pink gardens, and then to the outskirts of the city, to a cold, underground room by three shirtless young men lifting huge sacks of mail as the sweat beads down their chests. She is shown a shelf on which rests a large box marked "Poste Restante." A chair is pulled out for her, and as she sits, it creaks and tries to settle on unsteady legs. She moves to its edge and leafs though the postcards and letters. Some are as old as twenty years. Most have been opened. There are notes inscribed to lost Dutch travelers, envelopes addressed to Ann I Bodi, postcards with strange codes—perhaps pleas to or from drug-bearing kids long turned old and hard in mountain jails. She wants to stay there and read them all, to lose herself in the heartbreaks, but the men have work to do, and there is nothing at all from Juliette.

Keeping her promise, Anna scribbles Juliette a note and leaves it in the box with the others.

I am here. Where are you? It begins, and then she stops writing. Her heart sinks. What more is there to say? She has a feeling Juliette will never see this letter, just as the others had never read theirs. Anna had never chosen her friends wisely. How then had they chosen her? Perhaps by the accident of proximity that threw people together when they were lonely, or desperate, or adventuresome, or foolish. She couldn't say that she and Juliette were even really friends, though they were warm and cordial, full of attempts to connect. Anna had met Juliette through Seth, who was then a graduate student at Berkeley, and whom Anna would later marry. She always had a suspicion there was more to her husband's connection with Juliette than friendship, but it had never been discussed. He said he had met Juliette at a cafe he frequented near school; she made espresso there part-time. Drew little faces in the foam of the lattés. Enjoyed such a humbling task. Both women were artists; he thought they would like each other.

Both had studied Japanese *sumi-e* ink drawing, and it was not unexpected that they would someday travel to the country they'd seen so often in 19th-century woodblock print perspective. Travel, yes, but who would have thought they would stay? And who would imagine that Seth's death would have been the catalyst to a trip together elsewhere in Asia, and that Anna would be a widow at the age of 28? Fate had an odd way of winding itself around a life when you least expected it. If Anna had learned nothing else in her time on the planet, she'd learned that.

She was teaching kids art at a small children's museum, Juliette was living an hour outside Tokyo in a thatched-roof farmhouse, painting and teaching English to rural adults. They'd run into each other at the American Embassy's lavish Fourth of July barbecue, one of those welcome parties for newcomers, with a tent and a band and enough hot-dogs and hamburgers for the entire Army, which of course, wasn't invited. Anna had a vague notion of herself as a vegetarian and hadn't eaten a hamburger in years, but ended up eating two at the party. She hoped the protein might make her stronger, give her fortitude.

She had walked into the huge parlor with its shiny parquet wood floors, realizing she was standing in the very same room that General MacArthur had stood in, towering over the rumpled figure of a defeated Emperor Hirohito just after the surrender. She had seen the famous black and white photograph of the General in military regalia and the Emperor in formal tuxedo many times; now she stood under the same porticoes the General and the Emperor had once stood under. Laughter rang out from the end of the hallway, and she felt overwhelmingly sad. Those were times of war, certainly, but times of consequence. These were just times, she felt, that merely passed. Seth had been dead nine months, and her life had changed dramatically. Or had it? Before, Seth had decided everything. Now she had to make decisions on her own. Most of the time she felt strangely in limbo, hanging between worlds like a spider unable to finish spinning her delicate web.

Suddenly, Juliette appeared with a handsome young Austrian film-maker and a earthy-looking Japanese poet, one on each arm. Anna was drawn to Juliette, though jealous of her popularity. Juliette seemed honestly happy to see her, for she offered some sort of connection to the past and the comfort of the familiar in a foreign country. They talked of taking a vacation together in Asia after the rainy season ended. Thailand or even Burma were possibilities; they had three months to plan. Anna realized if they went in October, that would be the anniversary of Seth's death. She hoped that by going on a trip somewhere remote and unknowable, she could move forward. She could begin to put Seth behind her. She could finish that web.

But she missed him, still.

*   *   *

Seth had died in a single-car collision on a coastal high-way in northern California one clear autumn night. He had driven off the road, tumbling down a steep ravine near Muir Beach. The car had exploded when it stopped rolling down the cliff. Such an accident had only happened once before—teenagers on graduation night in 1967 who had had too much champagne. The police asked her: was it suicide? Did she think he had swerved to avoid an animal? She tried to imagine a deer or fox, or even perhaps, a humble possum, but couldn't. She knew that Seth would have hit the animal before he would have swerved. He always told her it was better to keep one's foot on the accelerator and drive toward the animal, who might be able to escape. Those who swerved usually ended up seriously hurt. She wondered if she could keep her foot on the accelerator if an animal suddenly jumped in front of her car. She doubted that would be her instinct.

He seldom drove fast, but the CHP report showed he had been going at least 65mph, which was highly unusual. Had he been unhappy? Was there something missing, something that if Anna had only known about, she could have given him freely? Or could she not give freely, and had she pushed him away? The questions haunted her, and she hated them for their typical-ness. These were the ordinary questions one would ask oneself at such a time, and although Anna thought of herself as ordinary, she had never wanted anyone else to be able to see it. She numbly answered "no" to all the policeman's questions. Then she collected eucalyptus branches from the site, gathering as much as she could carry, and putting them in a basket in her room. Over time, the pungent leaves had softened and wilted, their scent dissipating, dissipating.

Seth was thirty-four and had just gotten tenure. After

struggling for years, Anna had finally been offered a job as a lecturer at the same university. They had been married two years and Seth had become kinder, one day buying her a brand new paint box full of imported oils with names like Ultramarine Deep and Crimson Lake and Vermilion Tint. He cleared out the garage and built her an easel. He told her to take more time off to paint. They had decided to try and have a child. But then...

After the funeral, Anna applied for an artist's grant to visit Japan. Surprised that she actually received it, she quickly accepted, wanting to say "yes" to whatever came her way. Six months later, she had put her things in storage and had boarded a plane by herself for the first time, with no idea how long she would stay gone or how she would manage, knowing only a few words of Japanese. Not that she hadn't wanted to travel alone, but traveling without Seth would not have entered her mind. They were, as friends said, "joined at the hip." She bought the tickets; he held the roadmap. So it was in life.

One year later, when Juliette called after the Embassy party and suggested traveling to the remote Spice Islands, Anna immediately agreed to go. She had found living and working in Japan comforting when she finally stopped trying to act Japanese. Most people spoke English, and those who didn't were eager to try. She liked the regimented life she had there. For her it was much more freeing than the anarchy of Berkeley, where she had grown up at the height of the Free Speech movement and anti-war protests. Since she wasn't Japanese, she could let the structure hold her in, yet she didn't have to be bound by it.

★   ★   ★

Anna's hands shake from the dark Sumatran coffee, and the flight to Ambon is bumpy and frightening. She tries to settle into this newfound unsteadiness, taking deep breaths. Suddenly, she recognizes it as a place she has landed unnoticed months ago, alone for the first time and feeling it, after Seth died.

There are no direct planes to Banda from Bali, so she has to go to Ambon, where a tiny propeller plane will take her to this secret place where mace, nutmeg, clove had been grown since the fifteenth century. She had met a woman on the plane from Tokyo to Bali, a slight Indonesian woman with an educated British accent and the soft, knowing look of a spiritual teacher. The woman said her husband was a painter, but Anna did not tell her that she painted, too.

But then she said her husband had died, and Anna was struck by her openness. Or maybe it was that you could reveal things to strangers, lay bare parts of yourself that you were too guarded to expose to closer friends. Wasn't that odd? Anna suddenly wanted to talk, to tell this stranger everything.

"How did it happen?" Anna asked.

The woman, Urgan, spoke with intimacy and understanding.

"My husband had a brain tumor. He was forty-three."

"I'm sorry," Anna said.

"Don't be," Urgan reached over and placed her hand on Anna's, the pulse beating slowly on top of Anna's fingers. "I finally found the man of my life, and he was cheating on me. I kept wishing it would all just disappear. And then he did. How's that for gratitude?" she laughed ironically, looking up at the ceiling of the plane, eyeing God, then looking back into Anna's yellow-green eyes pointedly.

"So now I'm a widow. I get lots of sympathy," she said laughingly.

Anna tried to smile. Widow. God, the word itself stung. Like an old dowager. And yet, Urgan did not seem old, or even particularly alone.

"And you?" the woman asked.

"My husband died too," Anna confessed, telling Urgan the story of the coastal drive, the mystery, how much she missed her husband, how she is going to the Spice Islands to forget, to move on.

"Nothing makes any sense, does it?" Urgan held a white paper cup of tea, sipping it slowly. "When you come back through Bali, you must come visit," Urgan said. She had a large house on a black sand beach, where the wind sang at night through the open windows. She had an extra room, and a huge studio that had been her husband's, and lots of wonderful paint that had not yet dried up. She took out a piece of paper, invited Anna to Ubud, to her "retreat." She wrote out a phone number, which Anna took more out of politeness than intention to visit. She still didn't trust strangers.

Anna had forgotten about the note until now, when she unfolds it from the safe place of her wallet and holds it in her hands on the plane to Ambon. It is almost like an amulet. Maybe later she will visit the woman on her black sand beach.

Soon, Anna's plane lands in the small township of Ambon. She steps onto the dirt floor of a clapboard waiting room in a small, smoky airport, full of men vigorously doing nothing, and looks around. Anna is hopeful. Juliette hadn't been in Bali, but surely she would be right here at the airport in Ambon, and they would take the flight to Banda, and all would be well.

A thin man with neatly cut brown hair and sharp green eyes appears in front of her, startling her with his eagerness.

"Hello, miss? Do you need help?" he taps her on the shoulder.

"Yes, please," she says, "I want the flight to Banda. I'm meeting a friend, and..."

"The plane leaves only twice a week," he shrugs and walks away.

"Yes, I know. I want to take it," Anna follows him.

"Okay, then. Where will you stay?" He stops and looks confused.

"Stay?"

"Yes, a hotel. You will need one, won't you?"

"Isn't there a flight today?" her voice is edged in panic. "It's Saturday and my book says the plane leaves on Saturday. Look," she reaches into her bag and pulls out her guide.

"It does," he looks at the guide good-humoredly.

"Well, can you show me where to catch it?" Anna looks around the airport. No sign of Juliette, or any other foreigners. Just groups of men milling around, smoking, talking, sitting.

"The plane left one hour ago. The next one does not leave until Tuesday." He pushes his foot into the dirt. She looks at his legs, his feet. His brown corduroy pants are frayed and short. His rubber slippers look as if they are for inside the house only. The rubber are cracked and white in the cracks.

"What?" Anna thinks what all travelers think in moments like this: There must be some mistake.

"I think you will need a hotel. I can help you."

"What about my friend? Do you know who boarded that plane this morning?"

"I can check," he walks away slowly, moving with the understanding that there is all the time in the world. Outside, it has started to rain.

"Thank you," she calls out, flustered. How could this have happened?

"My name is Kino," he calls back without turning around.

Fifteen minutes later, he returns with a friend he introduces as Jimmy. Jimmy worked with him at the local Union Carbide plant. He is blind in one eye and wounded in the other, and walks with a dragging limp.

Jimmy takes out a flight log book, flipping its pages.

"Her name is Juliette Sands," Anna says.

"Right here," he points to a name scribbled on a line. She looks down at the page, and sure enough, Juliette had been in Ambon and had left this morning, just after she arrived. She had gone to Banda without her.

"Did she leave me a note? Anything?"

Anna's heart falls in so many ways.

"Sorry," Jimmy hands Anna the book to sign. "Next flight Tuesday. You should write your name here."

Fighting back tears, Anna picks up the pen and signs her name to the empty sheet.

"Come on," Jimmy says and he helps take her luggage off the conveyer belt. He places it by her feet. Wanting to offer a token of gratitude, she gives him a phone card, but he doesn't know what it is. He looks at it and flips it over. Kino explains to Jimmy what it is. She doubts he can use it here yet, but maybe in a year or two he will be able to find a pay phone in Ambon.

"This is our city," Kino takes a tattered brochure from his

back pocket and opens it to a proud, stark bronze statue high on a hill. It is Martha Christina Tiahahu, a martyred resistance fighter who stood tall against the Dutch colonizers centuries ago.

"This place is overlooking all of Ambon. We go?"

"Okay," Anna agrees. She has never heard of this town, knows nothing about it. It had just been a stop on the way to the Spice Islands. But now, it will be her destination.

"We wait until the rain stops," Kino says, taking her suitcases to a small room that is the airport cafeteria. They drink more Sumatran *kopi* with the dark grounds swirling at the top. Kino tells Anna that he and Jimmy used to work for Union Carbide in the battery division.

"Look here," he says, producing a right hand with a very short index finger and no thumb. Eventually his unit was replaced by machines and he was given severance pay. He'd spent the money on a taxi, which he'd been driving for two years. He liked it better than his other job. Much better.

She wonders how many such accidents there are in places like Ambon, and wonders if she should ask how many other friends of his have been injured on the job. Instead, she says nothing and waits for him to talk. He says nothing and waits for her to ask.

The silence is broken by the afternoon mullah, calling the devout to prayer. Kino is Christian, he confesses, and will not go for prayer.

The mullah is loud and plaintive, and the mosquitoes are mysteriously unquiet at this hour, so they stay inside. Most of the townspeople are out at the mosque, which Anna is not allowed to enter, being both a woman and a Jew.

Hours seem to pass before they walk out into the soot-filled street and stop in front of a small two-door Japanese car, rust creeping up from the underbelly and onto the doors. He loads her bag in the trunk, then walks around to open the door for her. She gets in the passenger seat.

They take off through the city. It starts to rain again. The rain spills into the car, and she understands why they have waited. There are no carpets, only metal punctuated by rusted-out holes as big as mangoes. She can see the road flying by in patches underneath her feet. She has never seen the road before in this way and it seems too close, too fast, too dangerous. She resolves not to look down again.

Outside the air is smoky, the pavements are cracked, the streets are full of pits and rocks. Wild dogs jump in front of the car, trying to bite the tires. Kino honks sharply at them, swerving, then accelerating.

"There!" he smiles as if seeing a movie star, pointing ahead to a hill. A large dome of the temple shines its gold cap over the ramshackle roofs of the town. They drive up a curving road to the statue. Gangs of small boys in dirty torn clothes cluster around the short, fierce figure of Christina, sword at her side. When they get out of the car, the boys rush up to touch Anna, frightening her.

"What are they doing?"

"They want to feel the hair on your arms."

"The hair on my arms? Why?"

"Something they have never seen!" he laughs, as if this is the most natural thing to do.

Then Kino seems to become jealous, and shoos them away. This only draws more of them into the game.

Anna holds her arm out in front of her. The boys rub the hairs this way and that, as if she were a dog. She turns her arm over and over. It tickles, and she begins to giggle, setting them off in peals of laughter.

"We must see Christina closer. We must touch her for good luck. Our hero," Kino says, pushing the children away from Anna.

"Christina. Christina. Christina," they chant.

Kino guides Anna closer to the bronze statue. Anna is a bit put off by his presumption. She feels she is being steered. Kino touches Christina's chest, the emblem over her breastplate. Anna does the same.

Kino asks the American her name.

For a moment she thinks of saying, "Isn't it funny? My name is Christina too," but she resists this impulse. It seems cruel to lie to the man.

She tells him her name, Anna.

What is it that makes her want to assume a new identity? No one here knows anything about her anyway. Perhaps that is it. She likes the anonymity of travel. That you can be anyone you want to be today, and become someone completely different tomorrow. That you can blend with a culture, yet still remain outside of it by skin and sex. She wants to be bigger than herself, a newly independent American woman, lost in a foreign country.

Walking back down the hill, she wonders how she will spend the next three days. She decides to hire Kino as her bodyguard and guide, offering him twenty dollars a day, not knowing if this will be a blessing or an insult to her new friend. She feels she can trust him. She feels he will look after her, protect her, even.

He accepts. There is only one problem. She must pay him, but it is Saturday and all the banks are closed today, tomorrow, and, in fact, on Monday too.

One last bank might be open, Kino says. He knows the manager.

★   ★   ★

Back in town, they sit on the stoop of the First Indonesia Bank. The manager has let them in, and Anna has cashed several travelers checks. Kino lights up a clove cigarette. His stomach growls loudly. Anna's is not the better for wear after the bumpy flight from Bali and the endless airport coffee, so they go to an open cafe and sit at a card-table with wobbly legs and no tablecloth. Flies swarm in the air above them. There is only one dish, *nasi goreng*, a kind of fried rice and egg meal, but it is plentiful and good and cheap.

They scrape their big spoons against the plastic bowls. He eats two bowls. She pays.

The sky is filled with a dirty, smoky film that makes the city seem even older than its years. She notices cars parked along the main road, full of men sitting and smoking.

"What are they doing?"

"Waiting," Kino says simply.

They go to a small pension, the Wisma Carlo, where jasmine hangs from the verandah and fills the air with sweetness. Tropical plants line the plain white courtyard and grow freely over into the path to the lobby. Anna sits down on a rusted red chair, pays for her room, and is shown her room.

"I will wait outside," Kino goes to sit on the stoop, lighting up another clove cigarette. She tells him he doesn't have to wait, because she will probably take a nap and not wake up until morning. He insists. Perhaps he lives far away and it is easier to stay here.

"No, you shouldn't stay."

"I don't have gas in tank," he explains, and Anna realizes she hasn't paid him for the day.

She hands him the ten dollars. He leaves and she is taken down a path to her room. The room is small painted a pale yellow. The paint is peeling and water-spotted but the room is otherwise clean, and the thin green bedspread smells freshly washed. There is one small window. The floors are concrete and cold. There is a plastic cup and a bar of soap, unwrapped, already used.

Unpacking her backpack, she finds two travel-sized bottles of Gilchrist and Soames British shampoo and body soap, courtesy of the Stonepine Estates in Carmel Valley, California, a place which couldn't be farther away in location or spirit from the Wisma Carlo in Ambon, Indonesia. Seth's parents had taken them there to celebrate his university job. They had been fighting, because Anna's first major opening was to be the following Saturday night at a gallery in Mill Valley. Seth said he'd be working late and couldn't make it. She pleaded with him to try to clear his schedule and come. He said it was impossible. She wondered why he couldn't make time for something that was so important to her. Just to show up, make an appearance, for her. He said she knew he loved her, so putting on an appearance was unnecessary. The way he saw it, she shouldn't care so much what other people thought. Didn't she know he loved her, supported her work, was there for her in spirit? What did it matter if he came to some opening? She tried to tell him that it mattered that he show the world his support, even if she knew it inside. He said she was insecure and immature. She felt the same was true of him.

That day, they shot archery on the Estates. Anna had not done archery before, but she focused all her energy into the tip of the arrow and directed it out into the air, straight to the target. At first, the arrow sputtered to the ground, but then, holding her elbow back and pulling the bow taut, it started to arc in the air, eventually reaching the target. Anna's arrow even hit the bulls' eye, and she felt thrilled. She was angry at Seth for his selfishness, and funneled that anger into hitting the target. She'd never done archery before and would never do it again. That night Seth sat in front of a fire in their suite and wouldn't talk. She cried, as if something unconsoled had been released with each arrow.

"Tell me what's wrong... " she pleaded.

"Nothing's wrong," he'd say. Then after a while, he'd say, "Everything's wrong."

She felt then that it was just the pressure of a full-time job, of facing a life with a career, responsibilities, pressures. Of having to grow up. Seth had avoided it for almost three decades, but now the world had caught up to him. And Anna herself was just starting to make a name for herself, was starting to exhibit her work in galleries, teaching, and feeling that it might be possible to live as an artist after all. That she could make it.

Now she wonders: Was that what made Seth drive away?

★   ★   ★

In Ambon, she washes her body, and the sweet smell of chamomile from the foamy lather, the brief luxury it afforded her once in life, seems wasteful here. How was it that those who had everything wanted more? Yet they could lose it all in an instant. Others who worked hard to gain something never approached it and had to suffer a long life of wanting more. She wonders if Kino wanted more.

Anna sleeps through the morning mullah, which drifts into her consciousness like an exotic poem. A knock on the door that wakes her up. Kino brings a tray with *kopi*, (coffee), hard-boiled egg, thick slices of white bread with red-orange nutmeg jam and a soft white cheese that resembles cream cheese but tastes like sour cream. There is too much food. She offers him some, but he waves his hand in front of his face and pats his stomach. He is thin, and she wonders if he is simply being polite. He puts the tray down and backs out of the room.

She picks up the cup of kopi and a piece of white bread slathered with nutmeg jelly and begin to drink and eat. Both are delicious. Kino comes back and leans against the outside of the door, waiting. He says he wants to take her to the archeology museum, before it gets crowded. Will it really be crowded with tourists in Ambon? He waits outside.

She dresses quickly and finishes eating, then goes out to the street to find Kino's car. For Kino, meeting Anna seems less a coincidence than a windfall, since when she gets into the car she sees that this new job has enabled him to buy more than gas— vinyl seat covers, a fresh bottle of gardenia freshener, still a full tank of gas, and even a hanging mirror ornament of Mother Mary. Twenty dollars seems to have bought a lot, or perhaps he has borrowed these things for the occasion.

It is hot, and the air is heavy though the winds are strong. A mile out of Ambon, they come upon two peasant women selling mangoes by the road. They wave. Kino pulls over. One, named Rachel, holds up eight fingers—she has eight children. The other, Sarah, smiles and pats her belly. Anna gives them her Japanese fan, inscribed with the words of Takeda Shingen, a warlord immortalized in *Kagemusha*.

You can do anything if you put your mind to it, is written in delicate Japanese script on the fan's folds. The women want to know what the ideograms, small eyes into another world, mean. Anna explains as best she can, and the women smile and sit back down, opening up a mango with a huge machete and offering it up to eat. Could they really do anything they wanted? Could she?

The four of them eat, sitting on the lonely road of single goats and absent-minded monkeys. If Anna were a composer, she would have been Chopin and the scene might have inspired a polonaise. She thinks of Seth, and knows Shingen's words are not true. Seth will never come back, no matter how hard she puts her mind to it. Yet, perhaps his spirit is here, hovering in the sultry air. She tries to imagine: If Seth were here, what would he do? Then the thought comes to her, startling her. Seth would never have stopped at the roadside stand. He would have driven on, anxious to get to the destination.

Anna has read something in the *Lonely Planet* guide about the *gua*, caves used by the Japanese Imperial Army during the war. She wants to visit them, and Kino agrees to take her there tomorrow morning. *Gua*, he says, laughing. He informs her that this is her first Indonesian word, since food words don't count.

Driving down toward the water, they see the most beautiful sunset, streaks of rocket-like red and orange shooting into the sky in Latuhalet, the farthest tip of the island. They walk amidst crater-like rocks and jetties, careful to avoid the crabs scurrying in the tide pools below. When it grows dark they return on the winding road back to town. Rachel is still sitting in the same place, fanning herself with the too-wise words of Takeda Shingen and waving like a schoolgirl as the Indonesian man and the foreign woman pass by in the dark taxi.

★   ★   ★

Kino is dressed in full camouflage gear and a white tank top when he arrives the next morning before daybreak. His body is tan and muscular, his skin smooth, and he still looks young, even though he says he is fifty-seven. He wears Ray-Ban-like sunglasses and carries a hunting knife at his side. This Kino is far more imposing than the gentle Christian Kino Anna had met at the airport. She wears shorts; he makes her change them. She should know this is a Muslim country, and she already draws attention to herself by traveling alone. She puts on long pants and starts to sweat behind her knees.

They take a different road that passes an ancient mountain village, a Christian village settled by the Portuguese in the late 1600s. The beautiful old white church is already full; an overflowing crowd stands outside singing "Amazing Grace" in Indonesian as the church bell rings out loud and sad.

Although the church is already full, the townspeople are still coming down the streets, dressed in their Sunday best. The men, mostly old, proudly wear crisp white shirts and striped ties and old brown hats. The women, mostly young, wear colorful flowery dresses and ballerina-like slippers. The girls wear hats and bows and smart dresses and hold the hands of their younger siblings. The boys wear suits and hats. Their feet are covered in patent leather, and they look grand streaming slowly down the old dirt roads. The older women walk barefoot, clutching bibles under their arms, dressed in long black robes, and follow slowly behind.

"Let's go inside," Anna says.

"No, " Kino says, "We'd make too much disturbance."

At first, Anna doesn't understand what he means. Then she notices that outside, the crowd has already missed a beat in the song—staring and gaping at this strange couple. She wonders if Kino feels guilty for not sitting at the pew, as he normally does on Sunday. Yet no one seems to recognize him. Does he attend a different church? Anna will never know.

They leave the town and drive more twisted mountain roads, coming finally to a dead end and a small dirt road. Chickens strut and peck, goats stand their guard. They park and walk down a valley, past crumbling tombstones and open houses on stilts, where women in sarongs clean their porches or sweep their red tile floors. They look up to wave and shout, "Hallo! Hallo!" then continue sweeping and singing as if nothing is out of the ordinary.

The caves at Kusukusu have not been traveled for decades, perhaps since the Australians routed the Japanese from their hold, Kino says. The entrance is very steep, and Anna stares at its depths, wondering what is still down there.

The gua had first been discovered by the Japanese. Three whole battalions had stayed in it, lead by an important general whose name was now forgotten. No gunfire had been exchanged, but Kino puts his hands behind his head in a pantomime of surrender. The Japanese troops marched out at the

Australian battalion's command, then there was an explosion. Perhaps they were hungry and tired, and had wanted to surrender all along. The general stayed behind and blew himself up with his hand grenade. Surrender was the ultimate shame. His troops betrayed him for their own lives, but had later died in a prisoner's camp of starvation. Anna had once been to such a cave in Okinawa, where the general wrote a suicide poem on the wall before blowing himself up. She wondered if there was such a verse etched onto the wall of this cave, sad words of farewell by a defeated man in a foreign country.

"Do you still want to climb down there? It will be cold, and dark," Kino warns.

"Yes," she says. She feels it is too late to turn around. She steps down first. He follows, holding her arm to steady her as she begins to slide into the cave's opening.

After descending the narrow tunnel, they reach a larger open area covered with dripping stalagmites. Their thoughts are interrupted by bat chatter, and the cave smells terrible, like rancid bird droppings and years of mold. They are still in a place tall enough to stand in, so they walk upright a few feet, until the path narrows. They trade positions—Kino goes first, shining the flashlight behind him to illuminate her path. She follows his lead, crouching down on all fours and slithering into the depths. They move this way on their bellies for how long? 15 feet turns to 30 feet turns to 75. She is cold, and suddenly scared. What if she finds a body down here instead of a poem? And what if someone else does, and the body is hers?

The flashlight's power seems minimal against this fear. Why had she felt the need to come here in the first place? Why hadn't she just turned around in Bali?

Soon the path is big enough for only one of them, so they crouch single file. Kino shines the light ahead, and Anna realizes that if the world were an unkind place he could hit her over the head and steal all her money, (which she had with her, since leaving it in the hotel would have surely meant its disappearance). He could rape or murder her and leave her here, where no one would ever find her. It has happened elsewhere, she knows. She knows, too, that it would have all been her fault for trusting a stranger.

She sees Kino crouched down ahead of her, his figure cold and uncertain in the shadows. The hairs on the back of her neck stand up. She places one hand in front of the other, sliding herself forward, following her guide. Her knees shake. She is sweating, small beads dropping onto the slippery ground.

Suddenly, Kino turns around and shines his flashlight on Anna, stopping in his tracks.He turns around and crouch-walks towards her. Her body stiffens with fear.

He holds out his hand and offers her the flashlight. She takes a deep breath in.

She crouch-walks a few steps forward, takes the flashlight and quickly turns around. He follows her out of the cave. They walk down the path, wiping the dirt and mud from their clothes.

He has given her the light, the one way out, the only semblance of control either of them had possessed. And she has taken it.

★   ★   ★

"What are you doing here?" Kino asks Anna as they

drive to the other side of the island, out to the Hito Peninsula to the town of Tulehu, with its silver-domed mosque and neat rows of cloves set out to dry on huge cloths by the dusty roads. The cloves will later be made into cigarettes and exported. As a teenager, she had smoked Guram clove cigarettes, their sweet strong taste numbing her lips and burning her throat, making her high for a short while.

She thinks about his question, realizes there is no right answer. "Enjoying my life."

This makes him smile. She smiles, too.

He drives slowly, as if enjoying the drive for the first time. He looks at his watch. It is only 11:00 in the morning, although it seems they had been in the cave for ages.

In Tulehu, teen-aged girls sit on the porches, legs out lazily in front of them, talking or singing. Their hair is in cornrows; they have egg white spread on their faces to protect them from the sun. All day long, they sit out on their verandahs, keeping an eye on the cloves, waving to cars as they pass. They don't seem to mind their masks at all.

They arrive at Waii (pronounced "why") another small Christian village, this one with a sacred waterfall where the women do their wash in the river, backed by a blue billboard of Jesus. "Jesus Swam Here" is written in Indonesian on the picture, but they have not come to see Jesus. They have come to see the huge sacred eel, famous for miles and just as long, swimming amidst the women's legs and the clothes they wash and ring out their laundry in the sacred water. Is this Kino's pilgrimage, or hers?

A smiling man slaps the water like a ringmaster to call the eels. When they gather around him he feeds them eggs as big as peaches. Though the eels are wider than his palm, he lifts them out of the water, one by one, for onlookers to admire. Soon they slither away and splash back into their blue home. The women continue to do their wash, ringing out shirts, skirts, underwear. The children run naked, screaming with delight each time the master slaps the water to call the eels up for show.

They pay the man for the show, then buy a cluster of red Raja King bananas from one of the women, and head down to the beach at Liang. It is about 25 miles from Ambon, and there are shipwrecks from the war. Wherever they go there are remnants of the war.

Kino drives to the farthest corner of the beach parking lot, and stops next to an orange and red van parked off-center, as if someone had pulled up to the beach at 95 mph and screeched to a stop.

A large family picnic is in progress at the beach. Kino rushes up to the party—the Hul Dasims, Kino's cousins, having a feast: fruit with spicy peanut sauce, fried cassava melon, banana pudding wrapped in banana leaves. The family laughs at how much Anna puts on her plate and eats.

The girls throw their babies into her arms and push their husbands at her side, posing them for pictures. Babies and uncles and long-lost cousins are dragged into the frame, along with the rather handsome young men, dark-skinned and shiny-eyed and glistening with sweat, who say they are either in the police force or the air force. The women all cook and take care of their children and work hard at home.

Anna is positioned in various poses as the girls snap away, giggling and talking excitedly to their boyfriends or husbands. One playfully pulls her bathing suit strap down. Another pulls on the pink ear of the small fat-bellied white puppy who wanders onto the scene like a daydreamer. He screeches and yelps. Anna too, feels happy.

Kino shouts something at the girls, which sends them into fits of laughter. He walks down the beach and returns balancing an old wooden canoe on his shoulders.

They dunk themselves into the cool water before paddling out into the blue sea. Later, they go home with the family, who live in an Army complex, in one of many rows of yellow-brown houses that all look the same and are the same, inside and out.

They play basketball on an old cracked court without a net. Hoop-shot, bank-shot, dribble. That is the extent of her vocabulary, which she exhausts quickly with the boys on the court.

They go inside to watch a spaghetti Western from the 1970s back at the family house, stucco and concrete and clean. Everyone wants to know why such shows are called "spaghetti." She tells them it is because the whole family sat around the TV eating from a big pot of spaghetti while watching them. They laugh, and say they want to eat spaghetti, too.

Kino, always busy, is now carrying buckets of water into the house. He tells her that she must wash her body. He points to the mud hut in the back. She doesn't want to waste water, so she declines. Kino proudly says they have plenty of water and that she should wash the sand off of her body. Defeated, she grabs the small white puppy as Kino ushers her to out to the room and deposits the buckets on the cold stone floors of a mud room in back. She looks for cracks in its walls through which they can see she. Why am I the only one who needs washing, she wonders?

She takes her clothes off and pours the water over her

body, bucket by bucket. Vanity, too, goes out the window. Even if they are watching, what will they see but a body. After all, it is just that, she thinks. Everyone has one. At least the dog will get washed too.

Later, they sleep in the living room on straw mats with rolled-up clothes as their pillows and nets as their blankets. There are nine of them in a room the size of a hallway. Heat from their bodies fills the room and makes Anna feel safe. She dreams of blue oceans, swimming in blue oceans, floating on the water, gazing at the clear sky.

⋆　　⋆　　⋆

It is a cold, pitch-dark, wretched Tuesday morning, and the plane to Banda will leave at 7:00am. They must get up early, to go back to the Wisma Carlo and get her things, and then drive to the airport. She cannot miss the flight again. They drive back into town in the blue cab with the dark cellophane tape over its windows—another new addition to the decor.

Kino tells her to lock the doors and keep the windows rolled up. There are many bandits and a taxi is a clear target, especially at that hour.

They make it to the pension, then safely to the airport.

By 9:00 the plane shows no signs of departure. Anna reads the Lonely Planet guide, having gotten used to, or at least better prepared for, island time.

There is a commotion as a large man strolls through the crowds, holding a briefcase and smiling in a relaxed manner. The people around him bow and move aside. It is almost imperceptible, but they bow. She too, feels the urge to bow.

"Who is that man?" She whispers to Kino, nodding her head in the man's direction.

"Iwal Sed, The Big Man. Grandson of a Spice Trader."

"Is he a politician?"

"Of sorts," Kino laughs. Suddenly, it is time to go. Everyone springs into action and all are called to board immediately.

She notices a blonde elderly couple, the first Europeans she has seen in a week, preparing to board.

"And them? Who are they?"

"So curious! I don't know. Dutch, maybe?"

Kino loads her suitcase onto the six-seater plane.

"Thank you," she says, "I can never repay your kindness." She reaches her hand out, but it is not enough. She feels she knows Kino better than she knows Juliette. They must meet again. She will have to stop over at Ambon to get back to Bali en route home. She will see him then, she is sure.

"Good-bye, Anna." He takes her hand and presses it gently against his lips, which are softer than she has imagined. It is the first time she has heard her name in weeks. Then he comes towards her, to try out a kiss. It is nothing more than a kiss—lips barely against lips—but for her it is like walking on the moon, and she feels light, full of joy and mystery, alive again.

On the plane, Anna sits next to the Dutch couple, who sit next to Iwal Sed. The plane takes off with a fast ascent, sending the box of coconut candy bars that are their snacks spilling into the aisle and scattering. Iwal Sed kicks them out of the way, then closes his eyes. He sleeps throughout the flight until they pass over Run, which the Dutch traded to the

British for Manhattan.

He points to the beautiful, lush island. The waters around it are completely still.

"Look," he says. "Quiet and peaceful. Nothing like Manhattan."

He smiles. Everyone is listening.

"Of course, we'd happily exchange it back. But America would be getting the better deal."

The small plane erupts in laughter and polite applause.

He closes his eyes again.

Tom says he had been a Dutch soldier in Banda in 1945, responsible for guarding many Japanese battalions. He could still sing Japanese and Indonesian songs. He testified in the War Crimes trials. He had retired in Lafayette, California, and wanted to return and climb Mt. Api—an active volcano, before he died. So here he was.

"Will you join me?" His wife, he explains, wants to make the climb but has an artificial hip.

"Sure. I would love to," Anna says, charmed by his courage. She has never climbed a mountain before.

Tom tells her he had gone to university but was sent to Brisbane military base for training. First he was sent to Java, then Batavia when the war broke out. Then the Japanese occupied Indonesia. They wanted to replace the Dutch with Ambonese. Tom's friend, a missionary who lived in Ambon and who encouraged Tom to come, was later killed by the Japanese. They had always planned to climb the mountain together.

Finally, they arrive at the legendary island, where the air is heavy and hot and the pace is slower than slow. You can tell by the way people lean to one side as they walk, floating in the hot air like a jellyfish in the ocean, being pulled along by the greater force of the waves.

Palm trees line the runway, and people wait under their enormous, drooping leaves, fanning themselves with their palms, drinking sodas, laughing.

Iwal Sed is met by seven beautiful children, who approach him one by one and wait for his affections. Are they his children? Anna wants to know.

He pats each on the head and kneels down to kiss their foreheads. He waves to a driver behind the wheel of forest green Jeep Cherokee, and the driver tips his hat.

Iwal motions to Anna; she follows.

The Jeep is soon packed with the children. Sed's staff tells Anna she will go to a bungalow on the beach at the most expensive hotel on the island. They tell her it is Iwal Sed's hotel.

Indeed, he invites Anna and the Dutch couple for breakfast on the terrace of the Wamalna hotel, overlooking the ocean.

They accept.

Wild, blood-red parrots hang from the yellow leaves of palm trees, calling to them as they walk to a long, rectangular table in the center of the tiled terrace. Iwal Sed sits down to the table, which is already set. He pours coffee for everyone, scoops spoonfuls of transparent orange nutmeg jam and spreads them onto slices of freshly baked white bread, handing one to each of them proudly.

"Our nutmeg. Hidden for centuries."

It is delicious. Anna thinks it is somehow like eating affection. They spoon a lot of it onto their bread and sip dark coffee. They talk about the Dutch, the Indonesians, the island's bloody past, its peaceful present.

"Yes, now it is peaceful. It was better with the Dutch here," Iwal Sed says.

"Why? The Dutch, they colonized...."

"You mean slaughtered..." says Iwal Sed.

"Yes, they...slaughtered the people," Tom says steadily.

"This is true, and it is terrible. But they brought money. We learn to forgive."

When Anna tells him she's living in Tokyo, Sed speaks in Japanese, Dutch, English and Indonesian. He then alternates to whatever the situation demands, even when it demands nothing.

"And why did you come to my island?"

She tells him about Juliette, their plan to meet, her mysterious disappearance at all the points of contact. She describes Juliette's height, weight, demeanor, even her clothes. Laura Ashley. Long dresses. Hair pulled back. Slender blonde with an innocent smile, the kind of woman Anna always wishes she had been instead of a short brunette with intelligent eyes.

"I left her notes everywhere we agreed on. I felt like a detective searching for a runaway," she says, her eyes sparkling, "And I wonder if she has been searching for me."

He nods as if deeply interested, although she has the feeling he is not even really listening. Then suddenly, Sed snaps his fingers in the air. Two bellboys appear.

"Tell them what you told me," he instructs her.

She swallows, then asks if they've seen a tall, blonde American woman.

They look at Iwal Sed for approval, then look back at Anna.

"She was traveling alone. Her name was on the passenger list, she must have come last week. Saturday, I believe." Anna adds She looks to Iwal Sed, who nods at the boys.

"No," they say finally, but she has the distinct feeling they are lying, although she can't understand why.

"Please think. Didn't you see a tall blonde woman?" Iwal Sed implores them.

They speak to each other. A child in a blue striped dress comes up and tugs at Iwal's pant leg. He bends down to kiss her. She begins to giggle and puts her forehead out again for another kiss.

The children are adoring of the big man and the employees fearful, it seems.

The bellboy who has been silent speaks up.

"Well, Sir, yes, But only one. On Saturday, there were two men and a woman, yes. A Dutch man and an Indonesian man, and a woman was with them. Tall and blonde."

"Yes. They think she was Dutch. Not American," his cohort adds.

"Yes, yes. That might be her? Where is she?" Anna asks.

"She is staying at the Lintz."

"Where?"

"A former Dutch pekenier plantation that is now a guest house," Sed explains, "It is just down the way."

"Call there," Iwal Sed orders his assistant.

He speaks to someone from the Lintz on a cellular phone and hands the phone to Anna, who is stunned to place the phone to her ear and hear Juliette's voice in this place as if it were the most natural thing in the world, like they are home in California. She fights her urge to hang up the phone, but the bellboys are waiting. By now, Iwal Sed has risen from the table, and the Dutch couple, who are actually staying at this hotel, have been shown their rooms. She sits at the table, eyeing the leftovers as she speaks. She reaches in her pocket for some bills, and leaves them for the boys. They glance in her direction, but barely acknowledge what she has done.

"Hello? Hello," she says again.

"Juliette, It's me. Anna. I'm here, in Banda. Can you believe it?"

"You're here? In Banda?" Juliette's voice stiffens, and she sounds proprietary, as if Anna has ruined her vacation by her arrival in paradise.

"Why of course. Just like we planned."

"Great," Juliette says without enthusiasm.

"I have been looking everywhere for you. In Bali first, then in Ambon. I looked for you everywhere. I checked the Poste Restante. You didn't leave a message. I didn't know where you were. I didn't know I'd find...."

"But you came here. You found me," Juliette says.

Anna holds the phone. There is silence as she realizes that Juliette does not seem particularly happy about her arrival, in fact seems as if she had preferred it if Anna hadn't found her. She is hurt to discover that Juliette has nothing to say to her resembling a welcome.

"Well, if you want to see me, come to Iwal Sed's terrace," Anna says tersely.

Anna hangs up the phone and gives it back to the assistant. She apologizes for the trouble, and asks them to thank Iwal Sed. She sits at the piano in the lobby and tries to play whatever Chopin comes back into her memory from childhood lessons. The piano is perfectly tuned; her memory is not. She always hated childhood lessons, something she had been forced to do. Now she tries to play the music from choice, from desire to hear it, not to please anyone else. She makes many mistakes, but the bellboys don't care and tell her the song is pretty.

Juliette arrives in an Indonesian *ikat*-dyed sarong in deep hues of brown and blue. She is tan and thin and appears to be thoroughly on vacation.

"Well, what happened to you?" Anna demands.

"What do you mean?"

"I mean, why weren't you in Bali? In Ambon? Anywhere."

"I'm here, aren't I?"

"We had plans…You said you were going to wait. To leave notes. To try and find me? Don't you remember?"

"I assumed you weren't coming," Juliette replies.

The way she says it makes it so final, and Anna wonders what part of her had given the impression that she would not arrive.

"Why would you think that? It was you who had to leave early. I would just as soon have traveled on the same day, left together, made the trip together," Anna says.

"Well, it's no big deal. Here we are. We still have a week to go."

Unexpectedly, Anna flashes back to Seth's perpetual complaint about her emotional state. She was hysterical, she overreacted to things most people just let go. She took a breath. No, she decided. She was not hysterical, she was not overreacting. She just had no idea why Juliette would not have waited for her, and why her so-called friend was so unconcerned about it now.

"But we made arrangements. We set meeting places, contingency plans. I never imagined you wouldn't wait for me at the places we agreed upon. I stopped at every one. You gave me your word. Why would you think mine wouldn't matter? Even if..." she stops herself.

"I just didn't think you would make it."

"That's all? So you left me to fend..." Anna is furious.

"...Well, I just thought you weren't going to join me."

"Well, I wasn't sure I would either. To tell you the truth, at first I thought I'd turn back, but I met a man in Ambon. Without him, I would have stayed in my hotel room the whole time, waiting for the next plane out."

"But you didn't. You made it."

"Yes, but..." she admits, "I was scared to travel alone. Did you travel alone?"

"Actually, I met two men on the plane from Bali to Ambon. We traveled the whole way together. A Dutch man and his Indonesian friend. They kept me company. They spoke the language. I forgot all about everything."

"Even me, I guess."

Juliette walks away. Anna couldn't imagine a person could be so cruel. She tries to understand what she had done to make Juliette so unconcerned, but she can't think of anything. She carries her suitcase and follows the tall blonde woman through the streets of Banda, scarcely noticing the beautiful buildings with their paint-peeled pastel walls and gardens growing deliciously overgrown in the hot, tropical sun.

Somehow, though, she feels vindicated. She has traveled somewhere alone, survived an unknown destination, and has met incredible people along the way.

★   ★   ★

At the Lintz Guest House, she meets Nawdir, a twenty-year-old entrepreneur who studies English and sings crooning love songs to no one in particular. He is trying to improve his lot in life by taking and making whatever opportunities come his way. Anna likes his drive, his ambition. He has so little promise to begin with, and yet he is utterly, completely sure that his hard work will win out.

He is the "host" and Anna's new guide. He plays guitar every night, teaches her the card game Patience, and informs her what to do if she sees a shark while scuba diving. (Swim toward it. Act like a turtle.) He is in love with being in love. He has a girlfriend in Ambon, but jokingly complains that she is not rich enough for him. Anna suspects the opposite is true. He is smart, and charming. She is sure he will find a way out of Banda somehow.

Now there are five of them, sometimes six. There is Anton, the Dutch journalist Juliette had met in Bali, and his friend Surdi, a handsome, naive Indonesian boy Anton plucked from a village in Timor who is also studying English. Anton is in love with him, and everyone but Surdi knows it.

They hire a boat to take them snorkeling. They see a turtle and fish kicked up into a cove, but so far, there are no sharks on Ali island.

Underwater, what they see: sad grouper, gaudy bright clown fish, angel fish, pink and red coral, sea anemones, wavy translucent plants, a very deep reef that just drops off into depth and bleakness. A barracuda.

There is talk of sharks, but no sightings. She tries to act like a turtle, sticks her neck out. It hurts.

Nawdir swims up to Juliette, his body touching hers, slip-

pery as a dolphin. She doesn't swim away. Anna watches
covertly. Back on land, they have a picnic lunch of rice, toma-
toes, cucumber, eggs and onions. They make her mouth cool
in the hot air. Nawdir smiles sweetly at Anna. Anna blushes,
then smiles so obviously in return in makes Nawdir blush. She
laughs.

Anna knows why the Japanese like to do everything in
groups. You can totally surrender, follow the crowd. It is a
nice theory, but not the case entirely with their group. Still,
the burden of decision is on all of them rather than one and
there's comfort in that.

They hike through overgrown weeds and half-hidden
tombstones to Fort Revenge, which the British built to get
back at the Dutch who had ambushed them during their colo-
nization of the island. Juliette has only brought high heels, and
holds everyone up.

They walk by a young girl plucking a chicken at the
entrance to the ruins. Behind the fort, there is more of an old
cemetery, where they find the graves of the Lintz family,
crumbled and overgrown with weeds.

They hike back to the beach, build a fire and fan the
flames as the sun goes down.

In Indonesia, the sun takes forever to go down, and it
burns.

Anna has Seth's ashes, which she brought to scatter in
beautiful places, scenic landscapes he would have liked. She
takes the pouch from her pocket and sprinkles some ash on
the shore as she walks the beach at sunset, collecting smooth
bits of colored glass and seashells. All of them are broken or
have a hole somewhere. Perfect seashells rarely wash up to
shore. They stay hidden in the water, while the imperfect ones
are always carried away.

★   ★   ★

That night Juliette comes to Anna's room. She sits on the bed and lights up a clove cigarette. She has a confession.

She inhales deeply, then blows the smoke out in a perfect stream.

Anna picks up the red cigarette box from the bed and takes out a cigarette. She lights it up and feels the thick, stinging smoke filling her lungs as it had when she was a teenager. Her hands are shaking.

Anna is the first to speak.

"You know what?" she says, "I miss Seth, but I have a suspicion I might be happier without him."

She checks Juliette's response. When there is none, she continues. "He was so controlling, wasn't he?"

"He loved you," Juliette replies.

"Did he?" She knew that Juliette had loved Seth back in graduate school, but he had made the choice.

Juliette sits down on the side of the bed, gathering her sarong around her. "Yes," she says. Her eyes widen.

"If you'd like to tell me about it, you can begin any-time." Anna realizes Juliette is still in love with Seth. Maybe she herself is, too. Is this what binds them?

Juliette draws on her cigarette, tells Anna what she has somehow already known. That Seth didn't have to work late the night of the crash. That he'd been with her, and felt so guilty about it he couldn't make love to her. "I told him to go back to you, to go to the gallery for your opening. He tried to appease you by making it. But he was speeding. You know the rest."

"Why did you do it?" Anna says strongly and evenly, not as a matter of pride or curiosity but just as a sad fact, like a broken heart or the love of your life, gone forever.

"We both wanted to," Juliette says, smiling coldly. "It wasn't the first time."

Anna takes out a knife from her pocket, stiffens herself with power and resolve, like shooting the arrow. She can't let Juliette hurt her anymore. She can't let Seth hurt her through Juliette. Her abandonment, her nonchalance, her complete disregard. Just like Seth. She was reliving it.

Anna backs Juliette up against the wall with her body and holds the knife to Juliette's throat, watches her tiny Adam's apple slide up and down.

"You wouldn't hurt me," Juliette stares into Anna's eyes, but her gaze is laughing. It makes Anna angry, and she puts more pressure to the knife.

"Not before. But maybe now. You deserve to be hurt." The knife blade rides on Juliette's porcelain-like throat, and Anna enjoys watching it move with her beautiful thin breaths. Breaths of fear.

Anna wonders why Juliette invited her on the trip in the first place. To abandon her? To get her revenge for the fact that Seth had not chosen her love? It doesn't matter anymore, Anna decides. Seth is gone.

She sticks the tip of the blade into Juliette's skin, like touching meat, testing the surface. It bounces back. Anna sticks it in a little more deeply, not quite piercing the surface. She could do this for hours, she thinks, like putting a paintbrush into a new color, experimenting with the palette. Somehow, holding the knife awakens in Anna a sense of passion. It feels good to be so passionate, and she wants to draw out the moment. She presses her knee into Juliette's groin, pinning her to the wall like a butterfly as she runs the knife tip up and down her throat steadily. She has all the time in the world.

Juliette begins to tremble.

"There's one thing I still don't understand. Why did you invite me here?"

"I never thought you would actually come. I really didn't."

"That's a lie. Tell the truth."

"Because I wanted to hurt you, okay? You had everything. I had nothing. Now we both have nothing," Juliette says.

Then she wrestles away from the wall, comes after her, hitting at Anna's chest, dragging her down to the floor. The two women fight like hungry dogs, tearing at each other's clothes, skin, hair, ripping into each other, crashing into the wall, rolling and cursing. Nawdir hears the commotion and comes to break it up.

Anna is smiling, her heart pounding. She has everything, and she will fight for herself to the end. She's never done that before, and the realization fills her with joy.

And then, she's crying because she's free. She can feel it like the humid air, reaching deep down to her marrow.

★   ★   ★

The next morning, Anna sits on the balcony of a beach house in town, drinking coffee from a glass jar, watching the waves. She feels as if she's cast off a skin, buried her burdens, lightened her life. She eats fried bananas and rice, writes in her journal, strolls the empty market, walks on the crumbled cobblestones to the governor's mansion. Once stately, it too is paint-peeled and falling apart, like all of the other houses in town.

She finds a French poem etched into the glass window of one of the bedrooms in a fine cursive script:

Quand viendra t-il le temps que foundra mon bonheur
Quand saunera la cloche que va sonner l'heure
Ce men que je reverrai le bard de ma vatrie
Ce sein de ma famille que j'aime que je blese.
Sept 1831

The signature is illegible. But a name is there. Even with her poor French, Anna discerns mistakes. Why had the note been written in French in the first place? Perhaps it was fashionable for rich nineteenth-century Dutch to use French, especially if they did not want their words to be understood, just as it was popular for upper-class nineteenth-century Russian, Swedish, and Japanese men to write in foreign languages if they could. These words could be read in translation as:

When will come the time that will form my happiness?
When will the clock strike the hour of the moment
That I will once again see the banks of my homeland,
The bosom of my family that I love and bless?

The day feels endless, the sky is sultry, the sea is the sea, stretched out before her. Anna views it through this window, through the prism of words written by a soldier or nobleman over a hundred years ago.

Finally, she returns to the Lintz for dinner. Tom, ever fit at 70, jogs through the streets, morning and night. He passes and waves. He has run marathons and even the notorious Dipsea Triathlon. He is sure the volcano will not pose much of a problem for him. Except for the fact that he has come down with the flu. Undeterred, he is training for Mt. Api, his final climb. They will make the climb next week. Anna knows she should be training, too.

The cook has made a papaya and string bean curry, and Nawdir serves Anna. She eats alone in the dilapidated court-yard as Nawdir serenades her on his guitar. Where is Juliette? she asks. She is in her room, door closed, reading, meditating, sleeping, who knows. No matter. Nawdir is worried about putting them back together again, like dogs who will go back for the kill. But Anna assures him it's over, that they've done what they needed to do. There's nothing left to fight.

Nawdir and Anna play cards into the night—Hearts? Betrayal? Solitaire for two? One game bleeds into the next, and the names no longer matter. Each of them has been hurt by love, and somehow, like animals, they can sense this shared pain. It draws them

Together. They're not cynical, and yet they know nothing will last. Ever. Not flowers, not cakes, not lovers. Only moun-tains and rivers and volcanos.

In the morning, there is a wedding party, the marriage of a local man's only son to a woman from a proud but poor family. The tourists have been informed beforehand and have pooled their resources; contributing 2000 Rp for a thermos set for the bride and groom. This particular gift was recommend-ed by Nawdir himself, and he even bought it with the money.

Indonesian weddings still followed the outdated rules and customs of dowry—the groom's family pays it to the bride's. The negotiations take place the day of the wedding, and they do not go smoothly. As it is, the bride's father is in an uproar—the bride being his only daughter and his favorite child at that.

The first half of the wedding is supposed to be held at the City Hall, where negotiations begin. Then the celebration is to move to the groom's parents house once an agreement has been made. Apparently, no agreement has been made.

They sit at the groom's house in a large room, decorated with pink and silver balloons, crepe paper in dirty colors like sand, photos of Mt. Api erupting in 1988. Mrs. Eva, the groom's mother, tells of how she thought it was her cooking that had exploded when the volcano belched its mortal fire. Her cousin, who'd once lived in Jakarta, knew better. He ordered her to run out of the house while he collected her jewelry. She gives a gentle nod to the Technicolor Jesus presiding over the Last Supper hanging on the opposite wall. Thanks to him, she says, I made it out alive. The long fluorescent light bulbs briefly flicker as the stealthy white lizards make their way up the wall toward the corrugated tin roof. The guests drink it all in.

A delicious spread is laid out on the table. Meats, fruits, breads and jams. The food can't be touched until an agreement is made between the families, so Anna and her friends sit in the folding chairs and stare at the food, smoke Guram cigarettes and drink cinnamon spice tea. Stomachs are actively grumbling by the time someone passes around a plate of pound cake and cookies of mace, vanilla, lemon rind, makanari and nutmeg, which are for sale by Mrs. Eva.

Time stops, freezes, melts.

Another hour goes by; the couple still does not appear. What has happened at City Hall? Apparently, the bride's father is not pleased with the negotiations, and does not want to move to the groom's house, so has corralled his family and the other wedding guests into his house, and will not let his daughter go.

Nawdir rummages through the 8-track stereo cassette selection. They listen alternately to Bryan Adams' "Cuts Like a Knife" and selections from "Hymns We Love," which features Skeeter Davis' "So you Know My Jesus" and Pat Boone's "Do You Know My Jesus."

After many songs of Jesus, the couple finally arrives. The bride has thick brown hair down to her shoulders, bright blue eye shadow and pale pink lipstick. Her face is weary, and she fans herself with a pink plush tiara. The groom is shimmering in a baby blue pinstriped suit, looking gangsterish and handsome. Nawdir pops the balloons in the doorway with his clove cigarette. A receiving line is formed. They all stand up and wish the couple *selamat ber bahagyan*, Congratulations.

The bride and groom sit center stage. They cannot hide their fatigue and do not speak to each other, simply stare straight ahead, looking bored and hungry. Mrs. Eva starts to eat from the table, and others follow suit. Nawdir jumps up, grabs a handful of plates, and hands one to each of the guests, motioning for them to get moving.

Finally, the bride's father storms into the room and demands that his daughter return home with him. The groom boldly grabs the bride's hand, telling her father that they are married now, and that she will stay here with him. The father storms out, slamming the door behind him. The bride bursts into tears.

Thus begins the first day of two weeks of wedding festivities on the small island.

"That was the worst party I've ever been to," Nawdir grumbles as they leave the groom's house and walk the crooked brick streets back to the Lintz in the darkness.

"Rather typical wedding, wouldn't you say?" Juliette smiles to Anton.

"How would we know? Neither of us has ever married," he says cuttingly.

"I thought it was thoroughly charming," Anna says. "They will have a good marriage," she says confidently.

Only now does Anna understand the value of struggle. She thinks the groom has been wonderfully gallant, standing up to his new father-in-law, risking his wrath. If he continues to stand up for his new bride, Anna thinks, the couple will be very happy together.

★   ★   ★

The next morning they all visit Mrs. Eva, as promised. Mrs. Eva's invitation has been more practical than hospitable, they see as she takes out her selection of homemade nutmeg jams and jellies and places them on a table in front of them to sample before they buy. Tea time finds them eating ice cream on her terrace and crunching coconut crisps coated with her sweet-spicy jam. It's as if all one does in Banda is eat or swim. They each buy a jar.

Tom jogs past the terrace, then stops to join them.

"Next Saturday night there will be a party at Fort

Nassan. Iwal Sed invites you," he tells them.

"It will be a party of generals, 60 military attaches and decorated war heroes. Live music and flowing drinks and a spectacular view." he says. "You must try to attend."

"After our mountain climb," Anna agrees.

They need a confirmed party of six to rent the canoes to take them to the island where Mt. Api is situated. Juliette will not come, although she had promised to join them. She says she is sorry, but she wants to swim with the dolphins. Tom is crestfallen. The trip might be called off.

"No, no, no. Mr. Tom, don't worry. We'll go to Api. I'll get Superman to help," Nawdir says confidently, and they all believe him. He has not failed them yet. If Juliette cannot climb the mountain, there will be someone else who can. After all, one cannot climb a mountain in high heels.

"Superman?" Anna turns to the young entrepreneur, curious.

"Yes. Or did you think I was him?" Nawdir's eyes twinkle at his own joke.

★   ★   ★

Saturday morning, Nawdir, Anton, Surdi and Anna wake at 5:00 and eat a hearty breakfast of *nasi goreng* and drink dark *kopi* before walking through the dark village to meet their hiking companions at the marketplace. The smell of paper burning drifts down the street. Someone has made a bonfire, maybe to grill fish for breakfast. The stray dogs are out, and the climbing party moves along the cobblestone streets, sleepy and excited.

Tom is waiting at the market in the stall where the banana seller sits. Together they go to the dock, where the famous Superman is waiting with Urik, their guide. Superman is young and strong and has a sweet smile and curly black hair, with green eyes like fresh-cut grass. Anna thinks he is extraordinarily handsome, and sighs. He wears only shorts, no shoes, no shirt. Two by two, they paddle a rickety canoe to the base of the volcano. Then Surdi has to paddle it back and pick up those waiting. The leaky canoes barely get them across the river. They are wet and soaked by the time they arrive at Mt. Api's base. Somehow, Anna feels that this condition frees her; wet to the core, she feels refreshed and alive.

The sky turns overcast, the air is humid, the pastel-colored colonial mansions take on a ghostly sheen when see from a distance, like the wings of moths. The sun is coming up. Anna looks at the scene, realizing it is a beautiful painting. She stores it in her mind for later, for when she will feel inspired to paint.

They start their ascent quickly, feet full of determination, trying to keep up with the Indonesian men, who climb the mountain quickly and agile in bare feet. They seem to be floating against gravity upward, as if being pulled up by a magnetic force that weighs the rest of the climbing party down.

It begins to pour. Two American colonels come jogging down the mountain, red-cheeked and soaked with sweat. A Dutch colonel follows shortly after them and exclaims, I'm so thrilled to see a woman up here.

She doesn't have the heart to correct him; they are still at the base.

They try to sing Japanese songs at Tom's lead. They

sound terrible, and Tom tells her it doesn't matter. During the war, the male population of Ambon was deaf. Many of them are deaf now, too.

"Why are they deaf?" Anna asks.

"They are pearl divers. The pressure of ascending too quickly made them lose their hearing. It is very sad, isn't it?"

"Yes, but they don't know how terrible the sound. It could be beautiful, couldn't it?"

"Song is song..."

"Indeed," Anna says.

"And here we are on the mountain, finally," Tom stops to survey the surrounding terrain, rust-red rock and steam and heavy rain falling. "It is so, so beautiful!" He begins to cry.

There are four rest stations on the mountain, small huts with bamboo roofs. At the first one they discover their guides have brought bananas and coconut cakes and water. After the fourth they attempt a grueling climb among rocks and debris from the 1988 eruption. By now it is a very hard climb, straight up.

Tom slips and falls on the way up, and lets out a sharp cry. Urik helps him up, and though a thin stream of blood runs down his bony leg, he is in high spirits. What Tom can't forget: when the steamship arrived, the Dutch flag was unfurled. The sight of it in the sky. To see that emblem of home so far away. It made him cry. To this day the memory seems as real as ever. He fights back tears as they climb, up and up. They reach the top of the mountain, soaked from the pouring rain. They have reached the peak at 1:00— six hours after setting out.

They peer over the crater at the summit. The sulfur emits steam that obscures the view even a few feet in front. It is easy to fall and the volcanic rock is sharp and jagged. Tom falls again at the crater, which is very hot. He lets out a short, sharp cry.

Anton, who had wisely brought a first aid kit, patches Tom up splendidly and sings Indonesian songs to cheer him up.

Anna walks over to the far side of the crater and opens the pouch over into the steam. It is so hot that her skin begins to break out in a rash. It is beautiful, watching Seth's ashes scatter and mix with other ash, much older than his. Anna watches the gray flecks float in the air. It seems like an illusion. Yet she knows this is why she really came, to burn her past in the ashes of purification and release, to give her love back to the earth and let it flow freely again.

Anton makes them pose for a group shot, hands clasped and arms raised in unison, as if they have climbed Everest. As if each of them had taken a lifetime to get there. In a sense, Anna realizes, she had. Anna fights back tears and tries to smile. When the last shot is taken, she breaks down. Nawdir tries to console her, but she tells him that no, it feels good to cry. She cries all the way down the mountain, holding the hands of her newfound friends. She feels the tears cleansing her, washing away her guilt and pain.

Kora-kora and gamelan music drift up from the island below as if from some other-worldy heaven up above the rain clouds. The musicians are practicing for the special ceremony of generals. The mountain-climbing party is excited to make it back down to celebrate. Rhythmic longing fills the air in musical notes that have no borders.

It takes three hours to get down, with Urik and Superman carrying Tom the last few miles. Two by two, they make it back over the river in the canoes. Filthy and wet to the core, they stop downtown to eat hot eggplant curry, chicken soup and fried potato and chicken dumplings, then go back to the guest house to clean up for the party, arms linked as they walk the streets in town.

That evening, Anna showers and dresses, heads off to the Fort, already full of dancing men and their solicitous wives. A band of Indonesian musicians plays beautiful gamelan music that floats in the air like a mysterious, erotic cloud. All of them, regardless of nationality or station, dance together in a big circle. Anna feels joy and belonging and the beauty of the night and the sky and only a little loss in the tropical air. Juliette doesn't show up.

"Why doesn't Juliette come?" Nawdir asks.

"Shall we go get her?" Anton wonders.

"Maybe she got lost," Anna says. But no one leaves to go get Juliette. When the party dies down, Nawdir begs Anna and Anton to sing karaoke at the Fongs' house, a large Chinese family of twelve, the only people besides Iwal Sed rich enough to have a karaoke machine, which Nawdir uses any chance he can get. Anna does not have the heart to tell him she hates karaoke and has managed to avoid it the whole time she's lived in Japan.

Now exhausted, Anton and Anna sit on the Fong's plastic chairs and drink Kool-aid from yellow plastic cups while Nawdir, erstwhile crooner, sings of unrequited love. Anna recalls that he has always sung along to the music piped out into the streets, songs of love and loss. Nawdir seems stricken by a sense of inconsolable and perpetual heartbreak. After all, he lives with the knowledge of inevitable partings. He hands Anna the microphone. She smiles, thinks some of his fatalistic romanticism can rub off on her. She tries a couple of Beatles' tunes, "Michelle" and more. She does her best, and it feels good to be bad and not care. She will be leaving soon, and she already feels it. Yet she feels she has been her, lived the week here as fully as she has ever lived before.

Meanwhile, the wedding has been called off, cut off in the middle of its first week, postponed indefinitely. The foreigners suspect it has been a sham, though no one cares.

Nawdir takes Anna back to his cabin that night. He wraps his body around her like a wave, and she is swept up in its power and beauty.

*   *   *

Anna flies back to Ambon, Juliette trailing behind her. She says hello and thank you to Jimmy Clipadda, who waves and pats her back, says that he is glad she has found her friend. Kino is there too, but he is sullen and hangs back in the crowd. Anna doesn't want to say good-bye, either. They have had too many good-byes. She waves to him from a distance, writes him a note and gives it to Jimmy, who promises to pass it on. She sticks a $20 bill in it, and then adds another. The two women board the plane back to Bali, but say nothing to each other the whole way. Anna feels expansive, light, happy. She never wants to leave Indonesia. She thinks she might move to Bali, somehow. She could teach English there. She could do anything.

They taxi straight to Nana's Cottages, traditional bungalows that feel extravagant and western in a luxuriant tropical garden with swimming pool and bar inside the shallow end.

There is even a shelf in the bar where people have left paper-backs.

Anna finds Marguerite Duras' *Summer Rain* in the bar, a book she has never read. She soaks in a hot bath for an hour, turning the pages. Juliette will take the first plane back to Tokyo. Anna has no plans at all. And she doesn't want any, ever again.

She remembers the note from Urgan, the Indonesian woman. Does she still have it? She riffles through her belong-ings, finds it folded up at the bottom of the bag, and still leg-ible. As she dials the phone, she wonders if the slight, magical woman will remember their meeting on the plane from Tokyo?

Urgan invites Anna to come for tea, to meet her daugh-ter Star at the international school that afternoon, where her driver will take her to Gianyar and bring her back later.

Anna takes the rickety shuttle to the lush suburb of Sanur, where she watches the children play amongst the palm trees in the school playground, thinking how easy things are in childhood sometimes. Friends play together, and go home. They meet again the next day, and play together, util one of them finds another friend, a prettier, smarter friend, one who likes boys as much as boys like her, and leaves the first girl behind. She spots Star instantly. A beautiful, odd wisp of a girl, like a figure in a Renaissance painting thrown into the twentieth century. The driver smiles an easy smile and opens the door for the child. They drive past stalls lined with golden buddhas glinting in the afternoon sun, stalls crowded with antiques, wood carvings and exotic painted animals. They pass villages full of people standing in the street, talking. They see temples with ornate golden roofs. Sometimes dragons guard their corners. They pass rice paddies, are intercepted by stray dogs, chickens, cows, motorcycles, bikes with loud brakes ridden by old men in sandals. Anna is no longer frightened, even when the driver tells her that the electricity has been knocked out due to a cremation of royals on the black-sand beach down the way.

When they arrive, it is just like Urgan said. The house's windows are thrown open and the wind dances in. Candle flames move with the wind, the waves crash outside. There are rich red Moroccan rugs and pillows on the floors, shelves full of ancient books and leather-bound diaries, photos in huge cloth-bound binders, and small tea-lights everywhere. Light is everywhere, soft and inviting. Urgan swings on a hammock on the back porch. Anna sleeps in a sixteenth-century Nepalese bed draped with mosquito-netting that cascades down its sides. She thinks this must be paradise, but by morning she has caught a nasty cold. Urgan comes into her room, bringing hot lemon juice and honey, sweet as a libation. That is paradise.

"I wish I could stay here forever," Anna says.

"I suppose you don't much like Indonesia," Urgan laughs, her lovely daughter close by her side.

Anna laughs too, because where they are is not Indonesia but rather somewhere north of the Elephant cave and west of the Monkey Forest, somewhere quiet and indelible. A house of women, close to the sea.

Urgan smiles and holds her daughter's hand, asks Anna if she will watch Star for a while.

"I would like that," Anna says, delighted.

"Will you paint with her? She likes to paint, too."

Urgan says that she is ready to go back into her husband's studio. He has been dead for one year.

"Yes, let's paint. Like children." Star giggles as Urgan

leads them into the studio, finding paper, paints and brushes in the wind-blown cottage.

Anna mixes soft pastels, feminine colors of flowers and shells. She picks up the brush and starts to move it across the canvas, soaking her brush in the sweet patina of loss. She knows that what she paints is not beautiful, it is not important, and it is not negotiable. But she also knows that it is hers: a map of her life, the one she left behind in a box marked "Poste Restante."

About the Author

Leza Lowitz was born in San Francisco and grew up in Berkeley, California. She has a B.A. in English Literature from U.C. Berkeley, and an M.A. in Creative Writing/Japanese Literature from San Francisco State. She made her way to Tokyo in the early 1990s, where she worked as a freelance writer and taught at Tokyo University.

Her work has appeared in *Harper's, Ms., ZYZZYVA, Yellow Silk, Prairie Schooner, Awaiting a Lover,* and in numerous magazines and anthologies internationally, including *The Broken Bridge, An Inn Near Kyoto, Prairie Schooner, The Atlanta Review* and *Expat.* Her writing has been broadcast on National Public Radio's "The Sound of Writing," and on NHK Radio. Her honors include a PEN Syndicated Fiction Award, a translation fellowship from the NEA, a California Arts Council Individual Fellowship in Poetry, an Independent Scholar Fellowship from the NEH, two Pushcart Prize nominations in Poetry, and with Shogo Oketani, the 2003 Japan-U.S. Friendship Commission Award for the translation of Japanese literature from the Donald Keene Center of Japanese Culture at Columbia University.

She currently writes book reviews for KQED Radio's "Pacific Time" and *The Japan Times.* She is also Reviews Editor for *Manoa* Journal, for whom she guest-edited two features on Japanese literature, most recently "Silence to Light: Japan and the Shadows of War." She also directs a yoga studio in Tokyo, Sun and Moon Yoga. She can be reached at www.lezalowitz.com.

Other Books

Poetry
100 Aspects of the Moon
Yoga Poems: Lines to Unfold By
Old Ways To Fold New Paper

Anthologies
A Long Rainy Season: Contemporary Japanese Women's Poetry (Vol. 1)
Other Side River: Contemporary Japanese Women's Poetry (Vol. 2)
(with Miyuki Aoyama & Akemi Tomioka)

Translations
America and Other Poems by Ayukawa Nobuo (with Shogo Oketani)
Japan: Spirit and Form by Shuichi Kato (with Junko Abe)
The Essence of Japanese by Gomi Taro

Editing
Towards a Literature of the Periphery (*Manoa Journal*)
Silence to Light: Japan and the Shadows of War (*Manoa Journal*)
Japan Journals 1947-2004 by Donald Richie

Non-Fiction
Beautiful Japan: A Souvenir
Sacred Sanskrit Words: For Yoga, Chant and Meditation
(with Reema Datta)
Designing with Kanji: Japanese Character Motifs for Surface, Skin and Spirit (with Shogo Oketani)